Laurie felt warm tears collecting against her cheek as she turned toward Ev and pulled her close. Feeling silly, Laurie had to adjust her own large breast with her hand so that Ev didn't roll onto her. More movements and shifting and they fit together nicely. Laurie found herself most comfortable with one knee bent and resting across Ev's. Ev seemed complacent with a leg wedged between Laurie's knees as she tucked her head beneath Laurie's chin and exhaled deeply. A shudder shook her, and Laurie placed a hand on her friend's hair, stroking her, whispering reassuring words and rubbing her back. Ev seemed to settle down.

During their college years, Laurie had never held Ev this way. It felt good to embrace a friend — this friend. She bet she could have held Ev like this back then, too. It would have been nice, rather like holding a needy child. But this was no child in her arms. This was an adult.

She dozed off, awaking from time to time. Ev hadn't moved. In a great burst of love for her, Laurie experienced a pleasant surge of warmth spreading throughout her chest, into her belly and radiating down her legs. It alarmed her, and then she remembered just who she was. She was the woman who was comforting her best friend.

City Lights
Country Candles

PENNY HAYES

THE NAIAD PRESS, INC.
1998

Printed in the United States of America on acid-free paper
First Edition

Editor: Christine Cassidy
Cover designer: Bonnie Liss (Phoenix Graphics)
Typesetter: Sandi Stancil

Library of Congress Cataloging-in-Publication Data

Hayes, Penny, 1940 –
    City lights, country candles / by Penny Hayes.
        p.   cm.
    ISBN 1-56280-195-3 (pbk.)
    1. Lesbians — Fiction   I. Title.
PS3558.A835C5   1998
813'.54—dc21

97-40425
CIP

City Lights/Country Candles is lovingly dedicated to my nieces, nephews, great-nieces and great-nephews and their great-great-great-great-great-great-grandmother, Shataykewainze.

It is further dedicated to those who have ever spent time in mental institutions, brave people to have withstood the demands placed upon them.

About the Author

Penny Hayes was born in Johnson City, New York, on February 10, 1940. As a child she lived on a farm near Binghamton, New York. She later went to school in Utica and Buffalo, graduating with degrees in art and special education. She has made her living teaching most of her adult life in both West Virginia and New York State.

She resides in Ithaca, New York. Her interests include backpacking, mountain climbing, canoeing, traveling, reading, and early American history. She has been published in *I Know You Know, Of the Summits Of the Forests* and various backpacking magazines. *City Lights, Country Candles* is her seventh novel.

Works by Penny Hayes

The Long Trail
Yellowthroat
Montana Feathers
Grassy Flats
Kathleen O'Donald
Now and Then
City Lights, Country Candles

Chapter One
Laurie, 1960

Joe withdrew himself from her and rolled over onto his back. "Ahhh, I could sleep for a week."

Laurie hoped he would, at least for the next few minutes. That way she could get up and go finish what he had started. He threw a hairy thigh across her hips pinning her solidly to the bed. In seconds, he was in a deep sleep, contentedly snoring. She lay still for several minutes before carefully extracting herself from his grasp. She loved Joe. He was kind and gentle and extremely considerate. He just didn't understand what made her tick. She rose quietly and padded into the bathroom noiselessly closing and locking the door behind her.

Sitting on the toilet seat, she touched herself, felt Joe's juices replaced by her own. What he had often spent an hour on, she successfully completed in seconds. Mechanically, without meaning. How was it possible for her to love Joe so and not go with him when he went, where he went?

She bit into a washcloth to squelch any sounds she might make. Joe would be devastated, should he ever learn this was how his lovemaking routinely ended: he in one room, she in another behind a locked door, trying to finish the job in one hell of a hurry.

There, done! God, the letdown.

She silently cursed between clenched teeth and stepped into the shower. Piercing needles of steaming hot water painfully beat down upon her until all of Joe, and her, had been cleansed from her body.

She toweled down until her skin hurt, then tossed on a sheer nightgown. Joe, still sleeping soundly, reached for her as she laid down her five-foot-six-inch frame. She patted his bristly cheek, kissed him lightly on his nose and let her weary body thoroughly relax.

She dozed off giving thanks that tomorrow, Saturday, she would begin her four-week vacation far from here, far from frequently nightly — and often early-morning and late-afternoon — disappointments. Not for Joe — she could fake anything when she had to — but for herself. Perhaps after vacation she would see a doctor. Maybe that was the answer.

She awoke to the sound of running water. The

bedside clock read 6:30 A.M. In a minute, Joe would bounce out of the bathroom, throw on a white T-shirt over his muscular torso, draw on white pants over powerful thighs threatening to split the seams and don his painter's hat at an endearing, jaunty angle on the back of his head, his black hair curling around the cap's edge.

Freshly shaven, his teeth gleaming, he emerged grinning. "Looking forward to your trip?" he asked as he finished dressing. Glancing in the dresser mirror, he adjusted the hat just so. He was so handsome with that early-summer tan he acquired each year, she thought.

She smiled. "Packed and ready."

He sat on the bed. "I'll miss you." With his big hand, he caressed her long, tangled hair that lay in a swirl around her head.

"You be good," she warned. Whether he suited her sexually or not, he was still hers.

"No problem. You too."

"Of course."

Brief words. A simple promise to each other. In the three years they had lived together, she was quite certain Joe had never cheated on her.

Flippantly, he kissed her on her turned-up nose and full lips as she closed her eyes. Her going was always hard on him. Because of it, he did not make this morning's parting kiss special. "See you later. Call if you like."

"I like," she said.

He left without looking back.

She lay back on the bed. "He loves me," she said. "Laurie Smith, you are a fool, missing a cylinder or two, sick — something." She wandered over to the

3

window and sat in a high-backed tree-branch chair, a lovely gift from her sister who had made it from small branches screwed together to create the rustic seat. Speaking to the pigeons perched and cooing on her fifth-floor studio apartment sill, she vowed, "I *will* see a doctor when I get back."

Following a quick breakfast of toast and coffee, she showered a second time, threw the bed together, pulled on a pale yellow blouse, loose blue cotton skirt — no slip — and heels. She tossed a few final items into her suitcases, closed them by sitting on them and then, with baggage in hand, locked the door behind her and headed for the garage.

Five minutes later found her in her new 1960 Pontiac with every window rolled down, the vents wide open, driving through early-morning traffic at its height. She tossed her head, swishing aside long chestnut hair that persisted in flying irritatingly across her green, gold-flecked eyes and oval-shaped face. She knew she should have tied her hair in a ponytail before she left. And she was already sweating like a dog even though this July fifth's temperature remained a cool sixty degrees. She hiked up her skirt until her thighs were barely covered.

In her ardent opinion, peak-hour driving in Cleveland was humanity's most lethal activity, and yet completely legal. Still, she didn't regret for a minute her leaving, not waiting in her quiet, peaceful apartment for the worst of the rush to pass, thereby saving herself a hell of a lot of aggravation. No sense in mulling over her decision. At this time of day, close-call occurrences were as common as pigeon shit, and if she couldn't stand the heat, then she'd damn well better get out of the kitchen.

4

The homey phrases drew her mind away from the countless cars, eighteen-wheelers, pickups and wild-eyed motorcyclists ripping by her as everybody dodged in and out of adjacent lanes while she, out of self-preservation, drove in the same berserk manner.

She couldn't wait to hit the open highway, couldn't wait until she saw the flat Kansas plains. She couldn't wait to see Eveleen and her family.

Lord, how she missed Ev. Oh, the wonderful memories they had racked up over the years. Best friends since their college days and sometimes, Laurie felt, closer than sisters, they had shared boys, clothing, class notes, money and secrets, some of which Laurie wouldn't have whispered to God. To this day, what Ev and she had done together most was laugh themselves silly. Each having graduated ten years ago from Stonybrook College in Pennsylvania, they still found enough about which to write almost weekly, and every summer Laurie spent her entire four-week vacation with Ev on her father's ranch.

There had been only one disconcerting time during their long friendship when Laurie had been worried, frightened actually, about Ev. Without explanation, Ev left school for three solid months. During this time, Laurie made frequent calls to Ev's father, Luke, and her grandmother, both of whom said that Ev wasn't up to taking calls right now and could Laurie call back. Then, just as suddenly, Ev was back, saying only that there had been something she'd needed to take care of. Although hurt by Ev's continued secretive behavior, Laurie refused to pry. Sometimes, when thinking about it, she wondered if Ev had had an abortion and it hadn't gone well.

It was remarkable that whenever she was with

Ev, everything was hilarious, everything was all right and calm. The only time she experienced peace in her life was when she was out there with Ev on that huge 150,000-acre ranch stocked with 15,000 head of beef, where her dearest friend now helped her father run the business. There, Laurie was free to ride the prairie, trip over rattlesnakes, fall off horses and chase rabbits on foot, an absurd thing for a thirty-one-year-old woman to do. She'd never caught a cottontail, had never come close; but, oh, the fun of turning too sharply as a coney tore by, of rotating too quickly in cowboy boots that were always too tight or too big or too uncomfortable, causing her to fall to the ground and skin an elbow or a knee. The sweet, delicious pain of it all, and of hearing Ev laugh at her until she too collapsed right alongside her in a gala of tears.

And all that unbroken sky ... And the strong, rangy smell of cattle and horses mixed with the sweat of working animals and cowhands' lithe bodies, Ev's not excluded, issued after a brutally hard day's work.

No, Laurie couldn't wait.

Her sweet, lovely Eveleen whose slim body stood only five feet two, who had remained a feminine woman even with working for years on the ranch. Her dark chocolate hair was long and thick, and her eyes were as blue as the Kansas sky and nearly as large; her eyebrows arched seductively across her smooth forehead. There was a small gap between her two front teeth, and against her darkly tanned skin, they looked snow-white.

A car horn blaring nonstop behind Laurie abruptly reminded her of where she was. She whipped over to the outermost lane where the truly frenzied drove and hemmed herself in on the left by a guard rail, ineffectually protecting her from the oncoming, maniacal motorists to her immediate right. She budged her car up to sixty-five illegal miles per hour in the forty-mile-per-hour zone, pushed Eveleen from her thoughts and directed her full attention on getting off this hellish highway.

Ecstatic to be leaving her apartment filled with books, tasteful furniture, expensive figurines carefully placed here and there, thriving houseplants and cleanliness — so much so that by the time each July arrived, the whole place reeked of boredom — she let out a mighty "Yaahoooo" and pushed the accelerator just a little harder.

She wasted not a moment considering all the problems that could possibly occur at the Cleveland Community College Students' Financial Aid Office where, during the ten years she had worked there, she had risen to the position of office manager. She didn't care if every campus in Ohio went bust, if every student refused to pay his tuition, or the girls, either, while she was away. As manager, she was entitled to forget the office for an entire month. And by gosh, she was going to do just that.

Forty minutes later, she was issued a speeding ticket. As soon as the police car was out of sight, she hit seventy, whistling a tune of what she imagined a cowboy in the saddle might trill while roaming the range on night duty, not slowing down until the need to take a potty break and refuel the car became an absolute necessity.

At eleven P.M. she stopped for the night at a hotel in Kansas City, practically staggering into her

7

room as she dragged her suitcases along with her. At the bar, she ordered an egg and olive sandwich and four tall glasses of cold orange juice chased with another two of ice water. Within the hour she was showered, in bed nude and completely happy. She had driven eight hundred and eighteen miles today.

She thought of Ev for a long time before falling into a trance-like sleep.

She imagined Ev walking toward her, smiling, welcoming her, waiting to hold her, to kiss her cheek, embarrassing Laurie and triggering an inexplicably strong, physical attraction within her.

Unconsciously, Laurie's fingers slid into an anticipating, warm, silky fluid glazing her swollen clitoris. Dreamlike, she moved her hand slowly as satiny heat heightened within her belly, threading itself along the insides of her thighs. She believed Ev was with her, beside her, on her, in her, until she became engulfed in a searing firestorm of euphoria.

She jolted awake drenched in sweat. For a few seconds she lay trembling in the darkness, staring at the shadows on the ceiling. "God, that seemed real." Embarrassment consumed her, as she said hoarsely, "I gotta get ahold of myself."

She went into the bathroom and splashed cold water on her face. It felt cool against her still tingling, burning skin.

Once more, she hopped into bed. Already, the dream was fading.

Tomorrow she'd make it to the ranch.

Chapter Two

At three A.M., Laurie's eyes snapped open as though strings were attached to each lid and given a sharp, upward tug. At once, she was wide awake, anxious to go, chomping at the bit — all that there cowboy lingo, partner. She laughed heartily, greatly amused by herself.

She lay still for only another thirty seconds before giving up on returning to sleep until five o'clock. A half-hour later she was back on the road, racing through a star-filled night and dressed in a white sleeveless blouse, light blue shorts and tan sandals, going for coolness and comfort; and her hair was tied back in a ponytail.

Excluding hasty potty breaks, fill-ups, tasteless pre-made sandwiches of ham and cheese and coffee to go, there would be no stopping until she reached the ranch this afternoon. Once on the Sunrise, daily she would consume buckets of home fries swimming in butter, thick slabs of ham or beef, golden mounds of scrambled eggs, heaps of pancakes and biscuits drenched in Vermont maple syrup, jams, jellies, a variety of fruit pies and coffee — hot enough to brand cattle, served in mugs huge enough to hold with two hands.

"Yehaw, eagle," she yelled at a large, sandy-colored, unidentifiable bird that flew across her path not twenty feet in front of her. It angled sharply upward, avoiding death only at the last second. She slowed down to sixty-five in chagrin at nearly killing an innocent creature, the self-imposed castigation lasting a full forty-five seconds.

As she headed southwest, traffic was minimal at this early hour. This route was once one of the lead-in pioneer trails to Independence, Missouri, and the beginning of the Oregon and Santa Fe trails. She considered for a moment those brave, hearty souls' rate of travel compared to that of her own. How far we've come in so short a time, she thought.

In the comfort of her swift automobile, she envisioned herself living a hundred years ago, exhaustedly walking or sickeningly bouncing along on a wagon pulled by mules or oxen, two thousand arduously difficult miles from Independence to Oregon and California. She thought about the Donners and their grisly, cannibalistic existence while snowbound for months in the high Sierras before being rescued, and the hundreds of unmarked graves she would pass when she crossed the Missouri border and into Kansas. This awareness disquieted her, and to lighten her mood she switched to thinking about Eveleen. This was no time to be unhappy.

Independent, cosmopolitan and very, very wise — that was Ev. Men who took her out quickly learned it. She was hell on wheels on a date, but she'd sent any number of hopefuls, disillusioned, disappointed or disbelieving, on their way.

"What the fools don't know," Ev had told Laurie some years ago, "is that Daddy's constitution is stronger than any man alive, and his chances of dying before he's ninety-plus are pretty slim. They're not gonna have any opportunity to inherit his ranch, if that's what's on their minds. Hell, Grandma McNelly is still living, and she's eighty-nine this fall with a brain still as sharp as a razor."

Grandma McNelly. That dear, wrinkled-up old crone was now one hundred and two years old. Blessed with remarkable longevity, she was Ev's great-great-grandmother. Between Grandma and Eveleen, with the exception of Ev's father, everyone else was dead, including Ev's mother.

The flesh on Grandma's body dripped with aged pleats from her face to her ankles, her flesh feeling like dry talcum to the touch. Her thin hair, commonly worn in two stingy braids encircling her head, was tenderly combed out by Ev each evening, the long white wisps resembling mares' tails, high airy clouds often the harbingers of a weather front moving in. She had not a single tooth in her mouth, often choosing not to wear her false teeth. Grandma's eyes,

11

black as pieces of coal, could enter a person's soul and know exactly what that individual was desperately trying to conceal.

Three summers ago, Laurie had had a serious falling-out with her mother over her living out of wedlock with Joe. The truth was that Joe *wouldn't* marry her no matter how many times she had broached the subject. He wasn't the marrying kind, he'd repeatedly told her. And she loved him too much not to live with him. As a proper Catholic girl and the last of her high school friends and college classmates still unmarried, she felt guilty enough (but not guilty enough to change her situation) without having to hear from her mother on how living in sin was *not* okay with her. What if Laurie became pregnant? What would people *say*? Laurie, who was still supposed to be a virgin, explained that she and Joe were very careful — he always used rubbers — causing Laurie's mother near hysteria. *She* did *not* want to hear about her daughter's method of birth control. Vacationing on the Sunrise a week later, Laurie gave no indication that their altercation still lay heavy on her mind, yet Grandma seemed to know all about the quarrel.

The two of them had been sitting on the dwelling-length porch after a late-evening supper, while Ev and her dad were busy in the barn checking a mare about to foal. In the dusky light, their rockers squeaked in mutual harmony. Happy for the moment, Laurie peacefully watched the night descend upon the prairie and listened to the nocturnal creatures' growing symphony in concert with the coyotes' howls drifting toward them from miles away.

"You hurt your mother pretty bad, Laurie,"

Grandma said out of the blue. "Y'all want to talk about it?"

Laurie looked sharply at her. "Did you call my mother?"

Unruffled by Laurie's tone, Grandma continued rocking contentedly. "Nope. Ev didn't either, in case you're wondering."

Laurie had been. Instantly.

Later Ev explained, "Grandma's got a lot of Kiowa in her, and those people just know things."

"How? How can they just know things?" No one could actually read another person's mind, Indian or not.

Ev shrugged carelessly. "Don't know. They just do. And if they want, they can die whenever they choose."

Laurie wanted to discredit that one, but something in Ev's tone prevented her from challenging such an unbelievable phenomenon. Perhaps that was why Grandma's longevity was so remarkable. Since no major health issues seemed to have arisen during her lifetime she was simply choosing to live on and on.

Maybe, Laurie speculated, Ev had this so-called ability, too. Often during their college years, Ev suggested activities they might do together, uncannily naming the very thing Laurie wanted to do. Thoughts that Ev might be tapping into her brain were seriously unsettling.

Her reverie returned to Grandma as she considered all that this wonderful centenarian had lived to see thus far: the Civil War, World Wars I and II and the Korean Conflict; countries rising and falling; women's suffrage and women joining the armed services. She had seen the nature of traveling great distances change from struggling across the earth by mule and wagon for months on end, to flying hundreds of people at a time, thousands of miles across entire continents and oceans in just a matter of hours. Grandma herself had come to Kansas by wagon from St. Louis in 1872. Further, there was the unimaginable gossip of sending a man to the moon before this decade was over. It would be something if Grandma lived to see *that*!

Grandma McNelly's greatest pleasure each day during the past couple of years, Ev had recently written, was sitting and rocking in the shade of the large ranch house's porch. She claimed she put more miles on her ladder-backed rocker than all the Sunrise's range hands did in a single day.

"Can't see like I once did, though," she had told Laurie last summer. "But I guess it don't matter. I had eighty-eight years to memorize it. Don't need to see it anymore. Now I just picture in my head what's out there. And, honey, I know every blade of grass on this spread."

Grandma was a great talker, and Laurie an excellent listener. She learned more about true western American heritage through the elderly woman's stories than she had absorbed in all her formal years of schooling. She would lean forward on the edge of her seat, just dying to hear Grandma's next words, her drawl soft as indigo velvet, skillfully unveiling yesterday.

The morning had grown hot with clear skies and the air biscuit-dry. Laurie had rolled down the windows before starting out for the day. Even with them wide open, the heat nearly knocked her sideways as she racked up the miles.

She guzzled cold bottles of Pepsi from a small ice chest on the seat beside her. "Ahhh," she said as she emptied another and placed it on the floor. She sang a little cowboy ditty Ev taught her years ago; her tires hummed along with her as the speedometer hit eighty-five.

At three P.M., she pulled up before the Sunrise Ranch's main gate, located just north of Centerview. Dust billowed around her, the strong wind casting bits of grit into her eyes.

The ranch spread out before her. Established in the latter 1800s, it had expanded over the decades until it was a thriving enterprise with sturdy barns, massive fields of grain, large fruit orchards, a huge vegetable garden and a stable of Thoroughbred race-horses. Located just west of the ranch, the family cemetery was girded by a wrought-iron fence. Several granite headstones already marked the passing of others.

A few domestic flowers and shrubs grew alongside the ranch house. Several windmills dotted the land. Fences encircled the main ranch, extending outward until they became tiny sticks in the distance, confining the thousands of cattle the ranch supported. Natural lakes, with ponds being a more accurate name for them, were only intermittently productive. That being the case, ranch hands had bulldozed out a few waterholes, their surfaces glimmering brightly in the sunlight. The terrain was so flat that even at this distance Laurie could take in the capacious sight at a glance.

Eveleen was waiting at the gate, straddling the biggest, blackest, sleekest horse Laurie had ever seen. The massive animal dwarfed his rider, making her look like a small child.

Ev wore faded Levi's, a long-sleeved denim work-shirt rolled up to her elbows, worn leather boots and an off-white western hat, the front and rear brim trained to curve slightly downward to protect its wearer from sun and rain.

Laurie leaped from her car. "You guessed my time perfectly as usual." Eveleen had never failed to be there when Laurie arrived.

Ev hastily slid from the saddle, grunting as she dropped to the ground. "Need a damn ladder for this beast."

Laughing joyously, Laurie grabbed her in her arms. They began chattering simultaneously, robustly slapping each other on the back. In their furor, Ev's hat went flying and her thick hair tumbled down her back as she kissed Laurie's cheek. Laurie held her at arm's length. "My, don't you just look the picture of perfect health."

Ev's eyes gleamed, her face seemingly lit from somewhere deep within and her happiness at seeing Laurie keenly obvious. "You've lost weight, you skinny old thing."

"Not much," Laurie answered. "Who cares, any-way? Let's not talk about me, my job, the East or any of that city stuff for a while." Her hands flew upward, her arms encompassing the sweeping land and sky before her. "Here, there are only earth and heaven. It's all I want to see, breathe, feel, think, taste . . ."

Ev laughed. "You're a cowgirl again. Do you say 'ain't' yet?"

"I've been practicing all the way here." Laurie walked over to the horse and petted his neck. "And where did you get this gorgeous animal?"

"Won him in a poker game last week."

"No!"

"I did," Ev replied, walking back to her horse. "Some wrangler I never saw before came in the Bright Lights Saloon up in Kinsley. Wanted to get in on the backroom action. First thing he said when he saw me playing with a couple of the local boys was, 'A girl? You fellas gonna let a girl play?' Both the men stood up and one of them said, 'She's already playing, bud.' That cowboy was pretty quiet after that. A real charmer, but he couldn't play cards. Too bad for him that he didn't know my daddy taught me to play."

"I remember the twenty dollars I left on the kitchen table one night last year." Laurie wiped the sweat from her face with the back of her hand. "Yes, you can definitely play cards."

"Horse's name is Blacky, by the way." Ev scratched the huge animal's throat.

"Bore, bore, bore."

"Name him, then."

"I can't name your horse for you, Ev."

"No one else is going to be allowed to try, but you can take a crack at it."

"I'll think about it."

"Get on him, Laurie. He's really gentle for a stallion." She picked up the reins where he had remained docilely ground-tied.

17

"Stallion?"

"He still has all his parts."

"I know that, silly. But a stallion." Taking the reins from Ev, she cautiously approached Blackie's left flank. "He's not going to buck, is he?" She had to stretch to put her foot into the stirrup but mounted up and straddled Blackie's wide back feeling as though she were taking her first dancing lesson and attempting her first split — and failing. "He's liable to toss me to the moon without any reason whatso —"

The stallion reared.

"Jesus, Ev, grab him!" Laurie felt herself sliding from the saddle.

"Grab the horn and hang on!" Ev yelled. "I'll catch you if you fall."

"Fat chance." Laurie's voice bounced out of her as she clutched the saddle horn with both hands. "Whoa, boy, down, Blackie, *down*!" The stallion bucked a couple of high ones, then settled to stand quietly again. "I've had enough," she gasped. Her voice shook. "Is he going to do this again when I try to get off?"

"Nope, just when you first mount him. Does it every time."

Laurie willingly dismounted and leaned against Blacky's side. Breathing hard, she said, "Call him Mr. Big Bucks, Ev. He's big, he's worth a lot of money, and he does buck. Expertly." She rubbed the seat of her pants. "Guess I didn't break anything. More time for that, later."

Ev retrieved her hat and dusted it off. Slapping it on, she said, "Come on," and sprang for the stirrup. "I'll follow you in. Dad's out on the range as usual, so you may see him later, but Grandma's waiting and anxious." She mounted the now Mr. Big Bucks; he reared, bucked twice and calmed down.

Laurie's heart leaped, but Ev handled the stallion as though she were deliberately provoking him.

"How's Grandma?" Laurie slid into her car, solidly closing the door.

"She's been waiting especially for you." A troubled look fleeted across Ev's face.

The Pontiac's powerful engine roared into life. "How come? Is she sick?"

"Follow me," Ev replied. She touched the stallion's sides and galloped off.

Chapter Three

Laurie kept pace with Mr. Big Bucks' easy canter as they traveled the two-mile drive to the ranch house.

"Hey, Grandma, Laurie's here," Eveleen yelled, slipping from the saddle and tying the reins to a hitching rail in front of the porch. At the door, she beat the dust from her body with her hat and stomped her boots free of grit.

Laurie brushed herself off as best she could as fine dust obstinately resettled on her. "Where's your grandmother?" she asked, following Ev inside.

They entered a dark, low-ceilinged living room. The familiar scent of leather, tobacco and sweat pleased her. It was as cool inside as the outdoors was hot. She breathed a sigh of relief as she tossed her pocketbook onto a big leather-upholstered couch.

Little had changed over the years. The house had a distinct male flavor to it, as though no woman had ever set foot in there. To the right of the door were pegs accommodating several hats. Laurie noticed that hers still hung in its customary spot, the farthest dowel, conveniently out of the way but still a part of the entourage. Lovingly, she removed the hat and ran her hand over its fine, expensive, brushed rabbit fur. The once proud brim and crown were battered out of shape from several past summers' usage. Deep brown with a rattlesnake skin band encircling the base of the crown, the hat was free of dust. Laurie knew that Ev tended it in her absence. She put it on and looked in a nearby wall mirror.

"Not bad," she said admiring herself and cocking her head this way and that. "Not bad at all."

"Very fetching — as usual." Ev stood close beside Laurie as she too studied her friend's mirrored image. Her eyes shone.

Uncomfortable with Ev's obviously strong admiration, Laurie returned the hat to its peg. She felt a need to break the spell Ev had cast over her.

She looked around, taking in her surroundings. The ceiling was still a plain white with exposed beams of natural wood. Cowhide and buffalo rugs were still scattered around the floor, and the dark wood-paneled walls were still embellished with antique Buffalo guns and Winchesters. Skulls of buffalo, elk, deer, coyote and even a fox were also

21

mounted on the walls. On a coffee table situated before the couch was a lifelike dusty, bronze Remington, horse and rider in an eternal deadly duel with a huge rattlesnake. A number of small tables of varying woods were set alongside four stuffed chairs positioned here and there. Laurie admired again the numerous pieces of dust-laden Indian artifacts and old bones, lit by kerosene lamps now converted to electricity. Periodicals regarding ranching, farm and ranch equipment, hunting and gun collecting further cluttered the tables and most of the chairs.

Off to the right was a long dining room, also heavily accented with masculinity by a cumbersome oak table surrounded with oaken chairs padded with black leather seats. Beyond the dining room was the kitchen, operated by Miriam and Pauline, two elderly, robust women who, for years, had served the family and seven permanent range hands, in addition to fourteen men hired during roundup. Pots and pans galore hung overhead. Two commercial gas stoves were kept operational throughout the day. Wall cupboards concealed dinnerware and utensils, canned goods and staples, and Laurie knew the refrigerator was stuffed with prepared salads and drinks. A large butcher's block filled the room's center.

Five small bedrooms at the opposite end of the house were sparsely furnished with double or bunk beds, fat pillows and woolen Hudson's Bay blankets. Each had a small table, a large dresser with mirror and limited closet space.

"Grandma's in bed," Ev said heading directly there.

"Isn't that unusual for her?" Laurie asked, following close behind.

"Very."

They entered the big house's most cheerful room. The walls were painted a pale blue, adorned with several large pictures of spacious prairies, impertinent flowers and laughing children playing around a watering hole while curious cattle looked on. Throughout spring and early summer, Grandma McNelly always managed to have a vase full of fresh sprigs of asters, gentians and columbines on her bedstand. On the mirrored dresser covered with a hand-crocheted dresser scarf were several bottles and boxes of perfumes and powders, a hand brush, comb and a few framed family photographs plus a picture in gilded frame of friends in Grandma's life long ago.

Eveleen strode quickly to her bedside and reached for her hand. She raised her voice a bit, saying, "Here's Laurie, Grandma."

"Good. Bring her over here."

Smiling broadly, Laurie quickly moved forward as the great McNelly matriarch struggled to sit up. "Hello, Grandma. How are you? Now, you lie back and rest." She bent to kiss her soft cheek then sat down beside her. Grandma released Ev, taking Laurie's hand instead. The old woman's grip was remarkably strong, Laurie thought as her fingers tightened around Laurie's.

Blankets covered Grandma to her chest, her arms resting at her sides above the covers. Her stark white cotton nightgown, buttoned to the neck, contrasted sharply against her decades-old, sun-soaked skin.

Ev adjusted Grandma's blankets. "You need to rest, Grandma."

In a crackly voice, Grandma replied, "I know, Evie, dear. Soon. I want to talk to Laurie some, first." She glanced at her newly arrived houseguest. Her eyes held milky pools caused by cataracts.

"I'll be here a long time, Grandma," Laurie said, reaching up and smoothing back Grandma's hair. "We'll gab for hours." Grandma's frailty was evident. Laurie had to hide her concern about the ancient woman's obviously failing health.

"Go on now, dear," Grandma said to Laurie, "and freshen up. "We'll have a nice long talk together afterward." She pointed toward the dresser. "Eveleen, bring me my drawing picture. I ain't looked at it lately."

"Sure, Grandma." Ev placed the gilt-framed picture on the bedstand. "Can you see it okay?"

"It looks grand there by the flowers, Evie, dear. Now go feed Laurie and let her rest. I'll take a quick snooze, too. Then you and me'll visit, Laurie."

"Of course, Grandma," Laurie readily agreed. "Sleep well, dear."

Hand in hand, Ev led Laurie to the kitchen to greet the ranch's talented cooks and to stuff her guest with their delicious food. "Hi, ladies. I got a woman here who needs some filling out."

"Well, look who's back," Miriam nearly shouted. For such a tiny woman, her voice could easily carry throughout the house and usually did at mealtime.

"Feed her hardtack," Pauline said. Her ample size betrayed her enjoyment of her own cooking. The cooks broke out in broad, beaming smiles at seeing their longtime friend, each welcoming her with bear hugs and backslaps that nearly knocked Laurie down. She backslapped with equal enthusiasm, barely making them twitch. "Sit right down there, child," Pauline said. "We've got all your favorites, so what'll you have?"

Laurie parked herself on a stool by the butcher's block. "Pile the grub right here in front of me and show me no mercy."

The cooks didn't. Forty-five minutes later, Laurie left the kitchen in terrible discomfort. Potato salad, baked beans, a slab of ham three quarters of an inch thick, cloud-light biscuits lathered with blackberry jam and consumed like bonbons, iced tea — the thought of it all made her ill.

Ev sat and watched her. "You don't eat much, do you? Easterners never do." She wasn't joking. She had put away twice what Laurie did and still had room for a couple of pieces of pie.

"I'll get better." Laurie belched. All she wanted to do was to lie down and sleep. Ev saw Laurie to her room. "I just need to rest for a while, Ev. I'll be more fit to be around by then." She gave Ev a light pat on the shoulder and fell face down on the bed. "Wake me in thirty minutes." She belched again. "God, I'm a blimp."

"Thirty minutes," Ev answered, closing the door behind her. Laurie could hear her laughing as she went back to the kitchen. Probably to eat more pie, Laurie guessed. She couldn't think about it. Soon she was sleeping soundly.

A half-hour later, Ev shook her shoulder. "You're sleeping hard, cowgirl."

"Gimme another half-hour, Ev," Laurie pleaded pitifully. "Thirty more minutes. I'm whipped." Her stomach no longer pained her, but her head ached like hell.

"Grandma's asked for you three times already."

"She awake so soon? What's the rush? I'll be here a whole month."

Two rooms away, Laurie heard Grandma calling. "Laurie Smith, you come in here. I wanna talk to you, girl." How could that old woman's voice be so strong, let alone downright demanding? she wondered.

"Crap," Laurie whispered as she hauled herself off the bed.

In the bathroom, she splashed cold water on her face and neck and counted the hours before she could lie back down again.

Grandma waved Laurie to a chair beside her. "Sit here, Laurie, dear." Ev was already in her grandmother's room. Wordlessly, she left them as Laurie meekly obeyed.

She asked, "Did you nap, Grandma?"

"Fitfully, dear, fitfully. Dreams kept jerking me awake. Don't remember what they were except irritating as hell. Here, give me my glasses." Laurie did as she was told. Grandma's thin bony hands with knobby-knuckled fingers slowly adjusted the wire rims behind her ears. The lenses were so powerful her milky eyes became owl-like and unrelated to the rest of her small face. "I been waiting for you, Laurie, girl. Glad you could make it." She was without her teeth, gumming her words.

"I always make it, Grandma. I wouldn't miss being here for the world."

"Why's that, child?" Grandma reached for Laurie's hand.

"Because I love this ranch and all of you so much. Especially you, Grandma." Playfully, she squeezed the aged hand spattered with countless liver spots and rubbed her thumb across the back. Ridges of protruding blue veins were soft and pliable.

"Good to know, Laurie." Grandma chuckled. Laurie, not understanding the humor in her reply, smiled as though she got the joke. "No doubt," Grandma continued, "this here's a wonderful place. House needs some work. Brightening up and such."

Laurie couldn't have agreed more. Neither Ev nor her father had shown much interest in interior decoration, but during her stays, Laurie frequently fantasized about how she would improve the house had she the chance, and the first thing to go would be the dead animals hanging on the walls and lying on the floors. But she tactfully kept these ideas to herself.

"Lots of history. Memories," Grandma was saying. "It's a paradise here, it is ..." Her voice trailed off as she looked toward the window facing the western horizon. The sun would be coming straight through it in another half-hour. The room would become warm, but not impossible to endure.

Laurie resigned herself to a good hour's conversation, suppressing a great longing to talk with Ev and the un- pleasant grittiness of exhausted eyes clamoring for sleep.

Grandma sighed and reached for the picture beside the bed. She ran her skeletal fingers along the gilded frame. "What a fine artist this woman was. She's the one who drew this."

Indeed, the drawing was excellent, capturing the features and, Laurie thought, the feelings of each figure. The ladies stood side by side dressed in fine gowns cut low and teasingly revealing. Behind them was a beautiful lake with tall, graceful weeping willows surrounding the shore. Laurie admired the portrayals each time she came to visit.

Grandma drew the picture close to her eyes and studied it for several seconds before passing it to Laurie. "I know you like history, Laurie. Real honest-to-goodness stuff. Not that nonsense they feed the schoolchildren nowadays. Nothing but a bunch of white men doing this and doing that and never asking nobody else anything about what they might think about it." Her voice had turned sour.

"It can be horribly boring, but if history is presented right, I like it. I love the way you tell it, Grandma."

" That's what history is. Boring. Always has been." Grandma looked again at the picture. " 'Cept when I tell it." She cackled happily. "Remember the time I told you about the blizzard of —"

"I sure do, Grandma. I remember all your stories. Every one. And they're all wonderful." But Laurie didn't want to hear any of them repeated this evening. "Why don't we skip the storytelling for tonight, Grandma, and you just rest? Really, we can talk tomorrow. Don't you think that's a better idea?"

"It's time to tell you about these ladies, Laurie. I ain't done that yet." Her eyes bore into Laurie's as she reached for her hand, clutching it with fingers that felt like bands of steel. The strength of her one hundred and two years seemed to pass to Laurie through Grandma's grasp. Her ears buzzed strangely as the grip grew stronger. "Now, this first one here," Grandma said, squeezing Laurie even tighter, "was Helena. Ain't that a pretty name? And ain't she just a fine drawer?"

Chapter Four
Helena, 1875

The day sweltered as thick air refused to move across the browning grass and drooping leaves. Intense sunlight expelled unwelcome blazing golden streamers across an undulating countryside. Heaven's brightest sphere, determined and steady, descended lower and lower behind tall, stately elms surrounding two identical, three-hundred-foot-long buildings facing each other. They were imposing edifices, three stories high with additional extensions off both ends equal to

the length of their frontages. A carriage drive and
wide slate walk led to the main entrances. The once
proud structures were now aged, worn by time,
weather and sadness. Created by good men for all
good intentions, the buildings had a pitted, decaying
look about them. Black iron bars guarded every
window. The ornately carved oak doors, designed to
welcome, were kept locked.

Beyond the main buildings were the waterworks
house, barn and cattle stalls. Attached to the stalls
was a large hog pen in which several fat pigs lay immobile in a half-dried mud wallow.

An inhuman wail suddenly blasted the serenity of
the place, and even the squirrels, who scoffed at the
day's oppressive heat by romping about the shaggy
lawn and playing tag amongst the bushes and high
tree branches, froze for a moment before resuming
their mad escapades.

Portly and handsome, bearded Jonas Heatherworth
McFarlane, well-to-do banker, well respected in his
community of Adams, Massachusetts, and known as a
man of sound judgment and strong religious con-
viction, pulled the buggy to a halt before the estate's
main entrance, the thirty-acre site surrounded by an
eight-foot-tall wrought-iron fence. On this ninety-
degree day, Mr. McFarlane's dark woolen suit hardly
bore a wrinkle and the man was barely sweating.

Jonas McFarlane was a quiet gentleman often
going long periods without speaking. But when he
did, his voice was soothing and controlled. This time,
however, his disposition touched upon the austere as
he said in a gruff, clipped tone, "We're here."

An attendant in a crumpled white uniform and

drooping brown felt hat studied the new arrivals through heavy-lidded eyes. He was badly in need of a shave and haircut and an upper set of teeth. He weighed a good three hundred pounds and rocked from side to side as he walked over to the high iron gates and swung them open on screeching hinges.

The bay drawing the buggy was bathed in frothy sweat, his normally clip-clopping steps deadened by the hard-packed driveway as Jonas drove toward the carnivorous-looking building to his left.

Helena McFarlane, Jonas's younger sister and the only child of seven still unmarried at the age of nineteen, clutched her brother's arm and looked wildly around her. She was by nature a happy woman with sparkling blue eyes and a broad smile. Her hair was the color of fresh butter. She stood five feet four inches tall and looked quite lovely in her blue linen dress and tan straw hat decorated with a blue flower.

"What was that scream, Jonas?" The awfulness of it drained her face of blood, turning her lips dead white and leaving her barely able to move.

Arriving at his destination, Jonas coldly shook her off and stepped to the walk. He extended his hand, saying, "Get down."

Helena gathered her skirt and petticoats. She exited the buggy unsteadily, still deeply shaken by the shriek she had just heard. "What kind of a boarding-house is this?"

"Get going." He put his hand on her shoulder and gave her a slight push. Eyes wide as saucers, she continued searching for the source of the scream as they headed toward the front door. Jonas pulled the bell cord. To Helena, its sound invoked images of dreadful happenings perhaps occurring within these walls.

Apprehension and fear began to saturate her as she glanced upward toward the building's tall roof and behind her at the equally ugly opposing building, at the fence penning her in, at the world just outside the fence. "What is this place, Jonas? It's not a boardinghouse at all. What is it? I thought we were staying the night and shopping in Lowell tomorrow."

An orderly clothed in a uniform identical to that of the sentry posted at the gate opened the door. He was large and frightening with a stalking, purposeful intent in his demeanor. Heavily browed with thick bones protruding outward over his eyes, he looked as though he were truly descended from apes. Helena had read an article about Charles Darwin's recent proposal which were causing no end of heated debates between modernists and religious leaders and sometimes invoking downright violence between the two factions.

"Let's go," Jonas spoke irritably.

She did not recognize her brother's gruff tone. He had never been brusque with her. Of the four, he was her favorite brother and she his favorite sister of three. They had shared many a secret from the others, playing tricks on them, gossiping about them behind their backs.

"Jonas, please. Let's leave here right now." She tugged at his sleeve, but he ignored her. The orderly stepped aside and grunted something akin to a welcome. As soon as they were inside, the door was closed, echoing loudly throughout the large foyer. She watched the man lock the door and swallowed a lump in her throat as she stepped farther into the capacious room. "Jonas!" She seemed capable of doing nothing more than to senselessly repeat his name while clasping his coat sleeve ever tighter.

Heavy, dark curtains concealed the room's four main front windows, dimming the hall's interior. Equally dark was the wallpaper, a brown background covered with darker tiny brown stripes. Various chairs and sofas were situated around the room. The high ceiling of hand-molded tin with its square-foot blocked flower designs was once probably a thing of pride. Now aged to a yellowing white, each block seemed to press down upon Helena's mind.

Behind a large desk blanketed with papers and files that suggested an industrious business was being conducted within these walls sat an efficient-looking receptionist.

"Be seated, please," she said. The uniformed man gestured to the chairs positioned before the desk. The receptionist, wearing a severely cut black silk dress with a prim white collar, her thick white hair piled atop her head, surveyed the new arrivals. "Welcome." Her piercing blue eyes peered over silver-rimmed glasses. "I'm Miss Buckley," she clipped. "And you are?"

Jonas briefly introduced himself and his sister. "Come, Helena," he said, forcing her toward the chairs.

Helena wheeled. She would *not* stay here. She would escape. She dashed for the door, but Jonas was too fast for her. Before she could take two steps, he had wrapped his arm around her, holding her so tightly that her shoulder blades pinched together. The brutish-looking man stepped in to assist, his dark eyes displaying an unnatural pleasure.

"I'll handle it." Jonas shot him a warning look.

The man's eyes smoldered as he backed away.

"Mama," Helena whispered. Jonas further tightened his grip, to protect her, she presumed, from this lout. But she did not feel safe at all.

Seating her but not releasing her, Jonas retrieved a document from inside his coat pocket. She tried to read the writing on the cover as it passed from his hand to the receptionist's.

"You're too masculine a thinker, Helena," he said. "It isn't a proper thing for a woman to be doing. You're ill and you'll be staying here from now on."

"Staying? Here? You're not staying too? But we're to shop in Lowell tomorrow, dear brother. I'm to buy a new hat and shoes and be fitted for a new yellow dress. *Tomorrow!*" An unknown future, a nightmare beyond imagination was being thrust upon her, enshrouding her senses. She felt she might swoon.

"There'll be no shopping for a while, Helena. The family has agreed. You will remain here."

At some time, she thought, there must have been a clandestine discussion regarding her. Some final decree. It was delivered in his voice and in his bearing. She did not know this man beside her. She said, "Why? For how long?"

"Father will decide."

"What does Mother say?"

"It's what Father says that counts."

"I am *not* staying, Jonas. This is not a place for ladies or for gentlemen, either, for that matter. Take me away from here."

35

"You're staying, Helena, until Father says you may leave."

"But I don't even know where I am," she cried. Hysteria welled up within her as waves of panic washed over her.

He turned to Miss Buckley for an explanation.

"This is the Massachusetts Hospital for the Insane, dear." She smiled, her face full of unmitigated pride.

"A lunatic asylum?"

Miss Buckley carefully read over Jonas's paperwork. "All seems to be in order. The doctor will arrive momentarily."

This time Helena did escape Jonas's grasp. She bolted for the door. Impotently, she yanked at the handle, intending to tear it from its hinges if need be. "Let me out," she screamed. "Let me out!"

As if from nowhere, two big men and two equally large women appeared, all wearing similar white uniforms, with the exception of the women's long skirts. They instantly seized Helena and led her to a chair some distance away from the front door, forcing her to sit.

"A tough case, sir?" asked one of the thick-set women.

Jonas did not reply.

At the desk, Helena watched Jonas sign his name to the paper that would admit her to the hospital. He ran a heavy hand across his eyes as his shoulders sagged. "I can't even think of today's date."

As though speaking to a simpleton, Miss Buckley clasped her hands on the desk and said, "July twenty-fifth."

He penned in the month and day, pausing at the year.

"Eighteen seventy-five."

Jonas gave her a withering look before concluding his task. Miss Buckley was apparently beyond caring what people thought of her because she never flinched, and Jonas was the first to look away.

A man wearing a long, crisp white coat over a gray suit entered the hall. "I'm Doctor Vendenti, Mr. McFarlane." He extended his hand as he approached Jonas. "We've been expecting you. I assure you, your sister will be in loving, caring hands. We'll look out for her. She'll be happy here." Smiling broadly, he looked Helena's way. "Won't you, dear?"

"No!" She fought like a rabid dog, but the others firmly held her. "Why, Jonas, *why*?"

"Priscilla," Jonas answered curtly, turning his back on her.

She struggled impotently against the strong, restraining hands, raging at him as he walked to the door. "What about her? She's all right, isn't she?" Nothing must happen to Priscilla. Nothing! Throwing back her head, she screamed as though to the heavens. "Papa."

Jonas returned, stepping close to her. She could have cringed beneath his stinging gaze, but she refused. His voice cracked as he said, "Papa knows. We all know. We think this is best. Frederick damned near killed Priscilla, and this family is no longer welcome in their home. That's your fault, you —"

Straining against her captors' hands, she yelled, "You had to be the one who told Frederick, Jonas. Why did you tell? It's your fault she was beaten.

37

Your fault. How could you do this to us, to her, to me?"

He wheeled toward the door and grabbed the locked handle. "Goddamn it, man! Open this door!"

The orderly snatched a ring of keys from his belt and quickly flipped through them. In seconds, Jonas was gone. The crashing of the door closing behind him pierced Helena's sanity.

They released her then, and she ran to follow Jonas. She was left to beat her fists against the unyielding door until in a drenching heap of perspiration, she fell exhausted to the floor.

Someone pulled her upright, then led her toward an entrance at the rear of the hall.

From somewhere above came a heart-wrenching outcry. Helena was barely aware that it was she who was doing the screaming.

Chapter Five

Helena would have collapsed, but she was delivered into the apt hands of a tall, heavy, uniformed woman whose strong arms kept her upright. Above hard, restless gray eyes, the woman's hair was cut brutally short; her facial skin from hairline to neck was pitted. Wire-rimmed glasses sat precariously upon the bridge of a severely narrow nose. A moustache darkened her upper lip; stiff white whiskers dotted her chin. Grasping Helena's arm, she pronounced in a gravelly voice, "My name is Mrs. A. We tolerate no nonsense here. None."

Helena experienced a sense of freedom dying within her bosom. It was as if Mrs. A.'s harsh hold upon her aided in slowly strangling her soul. Her entire being shook uncontrollably as perspiration continued to pour from her.

She braved asking, "Where are we going?" She received no answer as she was firmly navigated down a steep flight of steps and along a lengthy corridor lighted by gas lamps. Mrs. A. ushered her into a small room to the left. Once inside she heard the door lock. A white-washed ceiling and walls had since grayed with age. A few battered chairs, a single heavily scarred desk clear of even a single scrap of paper and a dilapidated reed wastebasket constituted the furniture.

Two female orderlies, both bullish and coarsely featured, waited expectantly in the center of the room by a large, galvanized bathtub filled with steaming water. Each wore her hair braided and pinned to her head. The taller of the two approached them.

"Here's your new one," Mrs. A. said. "Helena, this here is Mrs. Furant, and that's Mrs. Bostson. They'll be helping you."

"Helping me with what?" Helena continued to anxiously eye the tub. Were they going to drown her? Her arm was released by Mrs. A. only to be instantly claimed by Mrs. Furant.

"Bring her to Floor Two when you're done." Mrs. A. let herself out of the room.

"Take off your duds, dearie," Mrs. Furant said, still holding onto Helena. Her head seemed delicately balanced upon her long neck. Her eyes, pale brown with a splash of yellow and set too close together in her elongated face, appeared to look right through Helena.

"*I* will *not!*" With her free arm, Helena clutched herself. "No one is going to *touch* me."

Mrs. Bostson adjusted a pair of wire-rimmed glasses greased by sweat and sliding down her large nose. She looked with bored dismay at her companion. "Not another one." She moved toward Helena who was now reduced to a quaking mass of trepidation. "You do it, ma'am, or we'll do it. You have to take a bath. Rules."

"I bathed only this morning." Helena pulled frantically at the fingers encircling her upper arm. "Let me alone. I wish to go home this instant."

Both orderlies pounced on her. Expertly, they disrobed her and forced her toward the tub. Helena screamed and battled them and fought to cover herself, but clearly her captors had had years of experience at bathing the unruly, and next to them she was small enough to make their job easy.

"In you go, ma'am." Mrs. Bostson confined Helena's kicking legs. From behind, Mrs. Furant gripped her torso, locking Helena's arms around and in front of her body. Her breasts were painfully compressed beneath the aide's muscular grasp.

She shrieked as she was plunged into the torrid water. A large hand clasped her throat as another confined both her wrists in a steel grip. Someone began to haphazardly use a harsh sponge against her skin. She tried to scream, but nothing came out as she was plunged deeper into the water by the hand grasping her neck.

The room began to blacken, and strange sensations of being in heaven pleasantly muddled her thinking. She became detached from her surroundings and listened without caring to someone saying rather frantically, "Let her up, Betsy. She's turning blue. Christ's sake, you're gonna kill one of them one of these days. This one's clean as a baby's bottom anyway."

They yanked her from the tub, scrubbing her dry with stiff, rasping towels as she coughed burning water from her lungs and fought to remain upright.

She was soon re-dressed without memory of it. Additionally, muffs without fingers or thumbs were jammed over her hands and a three-inch-wide leather belt with a protruding metal ring at the rear was strapped around her waist.

Dumbly, Helena looked down at the brown waistband, not yet cognizant of her confined hands. "What's this for?"

"You're a wild one, dearie," Mrs. Bostson grunted as she drew the belt yet another notch tighter.

Her custodians escorted her upstairs with little trouble. At the second-floor landing, a thick door with a heavy lock separated her and her guides from the ward within.

Mrs. Furant said, "You'll be staying here." Exhausted from fighting everything and everyone since Jonas had first brought her here only a short time ago, she had no strength left to question anything and temporarily accepted her fate. Mrs. Furant reached into her pocket for her keys. She unlocked the door and Helena was herded unceremoniously inside.

Completely unprepared for the bedlam within, Helena staggered backward as though struck in the chest by a smithy's hammer. Her senses were remorselessly assailed by the scene before her, burning it into her mind forever.

Mrs. A. was there waiting for her. "I'll take her."

As the orderlies left, Mrs. A. directed her to one of several benches lining the galley, a long, wide hall. "Sit there and don't — you — move." She disappeared into an office a few yards away as Helena joined a woman already seated. Not seated really, but crouching upon the bench. At one time, the woman's eyes must have once held the sparkle of childhood joy, Helena thought. Now they looked deadened, sunken into her skull, the lids drooping and lifeless. She was filthy, smelling of urine and body odors, and her oily hair was a tangled mess. The dress she wore was in such tatters that one of the poor woman's breasts was completely exposed. She bore bruises upon her face and arms and what parts of her legs Helena could see. Dear, dear God in heaven, she prayed, is this what I'm to come to?

Farther down the galley other patients stood, squatted or sat upon the floor. Several seemed to be in various stages of illness. A puddle gathered beneath one of the crouching women.

"Let's go." Mrs. A. stood before her.

Helena followed the nurse, her eyes widening in terror as she passed by other patients. The faces of many were black and blue; some eyes were swollen shut; raw gums indicated teeth that had been punched out. Did the patients fight amongst themselves or had the staff done this?

A pretty young woman lay prostrate in the middle of the hallway, shivering and crying uncontrollably, begging to be allowed to go home to her husband.

She thrashed so that her threadbare dress had shimmied upward, leaving her naked from waist to toes. Nearby another patient lay immobile, encased in a corset type of robe made from rough tow cloth. Her arms were bound across her chest within the confining garment, leaving her helpless to use them at all. Her face was gray and her eyes saw nothing as she moaned continuously.

Dumbfounded, Helena watched as one of a number of orderlies — both men and women strolled the galleys — approached the inert woman. He kicked her in the side, shouting, "Shut up, you crazy bitch." The woman never flinched, never looked at him, but continued to moan as though nothing had happened.

"Leave her alone," Helena screamed. The man started for her.

Like a lightning strike, Mrs. A. snatched a fistful of Helena's hair, giving it a vicious yank. "Are you crazy? You keep your mouth shut." Helena screamed in pain. "We know how to handle things here." She released Helena, and a clump of hair fell from Mrs. A.'s hand.

There was a burning sensation on the side of Helena's head. She touched it and winced. Mrs. A. had snatched her bald in that spot.

Helena put her hand over her mouth and held it there as she continued down the galley, stumbling along beside Mrs. A., passing by doctors' offices and nurses' stations interspersed between many narrow, single-cell rooms, each secured with a metal door, its surface broken only by a tiny bar-covered window and lock. From within some cells came incoherent screams mixed with pathetic crying and unintelligible words. Fists beat on doors as accusatory statements of being falsely admitted to this godforsaken den of hell blended with threats of violence to all doctors, nurses and orderlies who worked there. The voices begged to be freed.

As they rounded the corner, the next ward looked and sounded no better than that through which Helena had just passed.

"It's the crib for you tonight, missy."

"Crib?" Helena looked nervously at Mrs. A.

"You can't carry on like you been doing and expect to be treated like a lady with her own room and all."

Helena weakly protested, "What about dinner? Is there not a dining hall here?" A bite or two might help revive her spirits.

Mrs. A. gave her a stern push forward. "Not tonight, crazy woman."

"You're the crazy one," Helena shouted back at her. "Let me *go*!" Pinpoint dots of white light exploded before her eyes as Mrs. A. gave her face a stinging slap. "Not another word out of you, lassie, or you'll find out what's good for you."

Helena held her cheek as tears gushed forth. She sobbed as she was ushered into a room barren of furniture, save for a box resembling an animal's cage, five feet square and five feet high. Like the tub, it too sat in the middle of the floor. Two female attendants were waiting to confine her within the small structure. One said, "In you go, ma'am."

This time Helena battled the aides as though her life depended upon it. She tore at their clothing and faces, but the mitts prevented her from inflicting any serious damage.

In the end, she found herself pinned inside the

cage. While one aide drew her spine rigidly against the rear bars by a chain looped through the belt's ring, the second strapped her ankles to the foot of the crib pulling the bindings so tight that Helena knew her feet would soon swell. So firmly constrained, she breathed only with difficulty. Though her hands remained muffed, they had mercifully allowed her arms to remain free. As soon as the cage was secure, Mrs. A. and the attendants left the room, closing the door behind them.

"No-o-o!" Helena screamed. She fought her bonds for what seemed a lifetime, then the door reopened.

Two uniformed men entered, one carrying a tray. Helena recognized the first man; he had met Jonas and her at the gate. "Hello, again, Helena," he said as he set the tray on the floor beside the cage door. "I'm Herman and this here's Martin. It's time for your medicine."

Helena looked at the tray. On it were a cup of brown unrecognizable brew and a wooden wedge. Why a wedge? Through clenched teeth she hissed, "I need no medicine. I need nothing from either of you or this insufferable place." Seething with hatred for the first time in her life, she believed she was capable of killing someone — *anyone* — at that moment.

Herman grinned wickedly, leaning close to her. "Now, darlin', don't be like that. You got to take this. Doctor's orders." His eyes were bloodshot, his cheeks heavily bristled. Strong garlic breath struck Helena. She became nauseous and swallowed repeatedly.

"I refuse to take it."

"It's for your own good, darlin'."

"Doing good for me would to be to let me go home this instant! And do *not* call me anything but

46

Miss McFarlane." She slapped impotently at the metal bars and tore at the tight-fitting mitts with her teeth.

Herman opened the cage and released her feet while Martin, a gaunt man with deep-set brown eyes, thin lips and curly brown hair, freed her from the rear bars. Before she could blink, Herman yanked her out and pinned her arms to the floor. He pressed a knee against her chest until she thought he was going break her bones.

He wheezed and grunted as he pinched her cheeks until she could no longer keep her jaw clenched, then he thrust the wedge into the side of her mouth with such force that two teeth on the lower left side of her jaw were knocked out. Without warning, he poured the cupful of fluid down her throat. She spit out the wedge and her teeth, coughing wretchedly and choking on the vile-tasting potion. She was certain that she was about to die. As she struggled to sit upright and battled to catch her breath, the men crudely fondled her breasts and crotch before easily propelling her into the cage again.

She was helpless even to cry out. The drugs they had given her had all but closed her throat. Laughing at her, they gathered up the tray and once again she was left alone.

She spat out as much of the medicine as she could. Tears glazed her cheeks and pain engulfed her mouth. She began to gag, but in time her stomach spasms slowed, then ceased altogether as drug-induced drowsiness took hold.

Chapter Six

Helena awoke late the following evening with her senses dulled and an unwillingness to give up sleep. Someone apparently thought otherwise. She was removed from the cage and freed of the mitts, shackles and belt by Herman and Martin. She behaved without an ounce of resistance. If she made no fuss, she might be out of here by tomorrow, she thought. She would also be very brave and ignore her swollen, inflamed jaw.

"Tame now, ain't you?" Herman said taking her arm.

Because of the drug's lingering after-effects, she was forced to rely on the men for support. Her body ached unmercifully from having slept in one position for so many hours in the tiny enclosure, and her feet unpleasantly tingled as her circulation returned. She replied without rancor, "I behaved foolishly when you were only trying to help me."

"You better behave, darlin'," Martin concurred, seizing her free arm.

She resisted the insatiable urge to claw his eyes from his skull and beat both men with the very belt she had been forced to wear. Instead, she presented them with a smile, hoping she looked and sounded sincere. "Of course, Martin." Her diffident willingness to demonstrate cooperativeness went unnoticed.

They delivered her to Mrs. A., who waited outside an empty room which was to be hers in the main wing. "In you go, dearie," she said. "And be quick about it."

Helena walked hastily inside, expecting at any moment to be struck for moving too slowly. Once past Mrs. A.'s threatening hand, she checked her watch, which by some miracle was still with her, and asked, "Must I go to bed already? It's only a little after seven."

"Rules. Everybody in bed by seven. Now, go lie down."

Helena lay on her cot and slowly closed her eyes, listening to the door click shut and the key turn in the lock. Her jaw ached terribly; she hadn't eaten in two days. She was a prisoner as surely as if she had committed some terrible crime and needed to be locked away. She had stolen nothing, had murdered no one. She had done nothing she would consider evil, nothing so bad that she deserved to be put away in a place of insanity and treated so callously. Yet, here she was, held against her will like a common criminal.

Inside the stuffy, confining cell not much larger than a horse's stall, with its dirty walls and peeling white paint, its worn floorboards, Helena lay unmoving. There was no furniture other than the cot and a metal chamber pot beneath her bed. Barred though it was, Helena thanked God there was an outside window.

Throughout the night, she listened fearfully to the unfamiliar noises of the asylum. Through the bars came the raw sounds of despondent women, women sobbing without pause, others screaming outrageously. Curses and promises of death to a variety of male adversaries — husbands, uncles, brothers and clergy-men — bounced off the walls and slammed headlong into her ears.

Heavy footsteps passed by her cubicle, stopping at the adjoining room where someone screamed without end. "Hanna," a deep male voice yelled. A couple of hard thumps landed against the door. "Stop your damned yelling and go to sleep."

For a moment, all voices ceased until a patient shrilly cried out, "Quit your own damned screaming, Jackson, and leave us alone."

Helena rolled onto her side and tried to block out the desperate noises with the thin pillow.

Memories of Priscilla obsessed her. She saw over and over again their last few precious moments together. The visions were so real, so painful that she clenched her fists until she couldn't straighten her fingers. She chewed on the insides of her cheeks until she tasted blood.

Beautiful, beautiful Priscilla with her lovely blue eyes and lips as soft as down feathers and breasts that Helena would have kissed nonstop for a hundred years, given half the chance. "Oh, God," she cried out and then fell into bottomless thoughts of her darling.

A small cedar-shake roof built atop the solid gray-stone well shielded a deep, deliciously cool, sweet-water pool lying seventy-five feet beneath the earth's surface. Weeds grew irreverently tall around the well. Saucy buttercups waved in the slight breeze. A heavily used path led to and from the house, barn and corral.

Helena sat on the grass, a slate board and piece of chalk in her hands. With rapid, efficient motions, she began to sketch Priscilla drawing water from the well.

Priscilla stretched to reach the wooden handle worn smooth and dark from sweat and soil of many hands and years of use. The simple cut of her blue-and-white-checked long-sleeved housedress protected her arms from the sun, concealing strong muscles rippling from wrist to shoulder. Slender hands, implausibly sturdy for so small a woman, cranked the handle.

"Don't go too fast, Priscilla," Helena said. "I want to get this just right."

"I'm not slowing down just for you. I want to get this over with. It's hard work." Priscilla lowered an oaken bucket into the well with a long hemp rope tied to its handle, the opposite end bound and wound around a crossbeam secured just beneath the roof.

She leaned over the well as the bucket hit the water with a splash. Unfettered by braids or ribbons, her long brunette hair fell forward, concealing her freckled face. Deftly, she gave the rope a tug tilting the container so that the water caught the brim and quickly filled to the top.

With an impatient hand, she pushed aside her hair. Her forehead, normally as smooth as a looking glass, strained with the effort of raising the cumbersome vessel. She ran her sleeve across her face, the fabric absorbing the salty moisture running into her eyes and drenching her full lips and petite chin.

Helena watched the veins on the backs of her lover's hands thicken and fill with blood as she reeled up the weighty bucket. She grunted with the effort it took to bring it up.

Priscilla quickly set the safety catch on the handle so that the bucket wouldn't plummet below. Only five feet tall, she had to stretch to swing it onto the well's edge. She freed it, the container splashing a few drops against her leg. She laughed musically as Helena smiled at her, amused by Priscilla's stubbornness that she alone would draw the water without any of Helena's help, thank you.

Helena leaped up. "What do you think?" She displayed her work.

Priscilla smiled and put down the heavy container. She took the slate from Helena's hand. The flowers and buildings were there. The well was there, too. But overlaying this busy background was the face of

Priscilla. "It looks exactly like me. How can you draw like that?"

"Don't know. You want it?"

"Do you have more slate?"

"Piles. My family thinks I'm crazy for wasting my time like this."

Priscilla handed back the picture and started for the house, bucket in hand. "Well, you're not. Too bad you can't draw for a living. You'd do well."

"But only if I could sell my work."

"I think we'd better be thinking of the work that's to be done right now," Priscilla said, shifting the bucket to her left side, "and make sure everything is ready."

It was cool inside the stone house, its thick walls holding back the unusually hot summer sun. Massachusetts had seldom experienced such blistering weather. Even the cows didn't seem to have energy enough to moo as they stood beneath the shady willow trees growing along the creek bank, their hooves in the water.

Helena took the bucket from Priscilla and placed it in the dry sink.

Helena's mother loved making hay, loved the hard, physical demands upon her body, the sun burning her face and hands. Yearly, she accompanied Father and his field hands to the meadows. Both her parents, three hired hands and Priscilla's husband, Frederick, were working in the far north field while she and Priscilla stayed behind to prepare a big meal everybody could fill up on and not have to think about eating again before breakfast time.

Four freshly killed and plucked chickens and two

dozen large potatoes slowly baked in the wood-oven. Just before Helena sounded the call for dinner, she would put in the biscuits. In addition, vegetable soup simmered on the stove. This morning's milking cooled in the milkhouse; cream had been churned earlier so there would be fresh butter for the biscuits and sweetened cream for three strawberry-rhubarb pies and one dried-apple pie already set out to cool on the table. Supper would be served in two hours. For two hours she would be alone with Priscilla. A lifetime.

After checking that all was well, Helena took Priscilla's hand and led the way to her upstairs bedroom. They had been lovers for the past two years and content with their arrangement of seeing each other when they could. Laughing, they fell upon the thick down blankets, rolling each other over and over, back and forth. Their lips locked and their teeth clicked together as they opened their mouths wide and bathed each other with warm wet tongues.

When they broke apart, Priscilla whispered, "It's so much better with you, my darling. So much better than with Fred —"

Helena covered Priscilla's mouth with her own, moaning with heat. She threw herself over Priscilla, yanking up the skirts of their dresses.

Heat emanated upward from Priscilla's closed thighs. Helena slid a hand between them. "Open your legs, lovely one."

Priscilla did and Helena readily buried her face in Priscilla's hair, her heat, her moisture. How she loved this woman, honored her, adored her.

Priscilla began to arch as Helena's tongue caressed her. She became wetter, if it were possible. She pushed hard against her lover's mouth, crying out her love for Helena. Helena stayed with her until Priscilla was thrashing from side to side with Helena's head clenched between her legs.

Helena waited until Priscilla released her, then moved to sit lightly upon her chest. Priscilla put her hands on Helena's bottom and drew her to her mouth. Helena felt Priscilla's tongue pressing against her, entering her, sucking on her. She was sure she was going to go mad with desire as Priscilla's tongue stroked her. She was overcome with rapture as she held her position. A powerful climax gripped her and her breathing became labored and loud.

Neither she nor Priscilla heard the kitchen door open.

Chapter Seven

At 6:30 A.M., patients were roused for medications and breakfast. Helena's lock rattled and the door swung open.

"Morning, Miss McFarlane. My name's Millie. I bring folks their meals on this floor." A woman — and thank God she wasn't big — with a bright shining face held a bowl of gruel and a glass of milk in her hands. Her uniform was crisp and clean, and she wore a big smile, something seemingly unsuited for this institution. "You get cereal this morning." A male orderly waited at the door — no doubt an extra hand if Helena behaved badly.

"Morning," Helena muttered. She sat up and took the bowl. A spoon stood straight up in the center of its contents. As hungry as she was the food looked as disgusting as pig brains.

Millie glanced around the cubic. "A couple of rules for you to know," she said. "Can you make your own bed?" Helena nodded. "That's good. So many who come here can't. Or won't. Your room will be checked each day, so you want to see to it that you keep it tidy."

Helena looked at Millie to see if she were joking. She wasn't. And how could she not be tidy? She had only the clothing on her back to consider. And how too was she to go about washing her clothes? But perhaps that didn't happen here.

As she stared again at her breakfast, she asked, "Can any of these women do anything for themselves?"

"Oh, my, yes. So many are so smart and book learned. Some sing and some play the piano. But we don't have a piano here. They just told me they could."

"Then why are they here?"

"Oh, I can't talk about that. That's confidential."

"Can you talk about why I'm here?"

"You'll just have to wait till the doctor sees you. He'll explain everything." She moved to look out Helena's window. "You got a pretty view here. You're lucky." Facing Helena, she said, "I can tell you that folks who live on this floor can't leave their rooms without full supervision."

"But the ladies I saw yesterday in the galley . . ."

"They're safe. Don't know about you yet."

"But I'm not one bit crazy. Not one bit." Helena's voice began to rise.

"Oh, you'll have to ask your doctor about that."

"I'd like to ask him right now, if you please."

"I'm afraid you won't be seeing him for a while. He's gone home for a little holiday. But I'll be sure to let him know you're here when he gets back."

Helena steadied her tone. "It seems as though he would want to see me right away. I am a new patient here."

"You'll see him plenty. Don't worry about that. Just be sure to eat and rest, now. That's your job." Millie began to unnecessarily fluff Helena's pillow that didn't fluff a bit. Helena had tried several times during the night. "Keep yourself together and you'll go to the dining hall right away and be moved to the third floor, too. It's pure freedom up there compared to here. Dormitories and such."

Helena asked, "Do those ladies I saw in the galley yesterday eat here or in the dining hall?"

"Dining hall."

"Then why must I eat here? They look to be in worse shape than me." And she certainly didn't consider herself to be in any kind of bad shape at all.

Millie continued fussing with the cot. Speaking quietly, she said, "Everybody starts out here, or in the cage. That is, unless you got somebody on the outside willing to pay extra for you. Then you get special treatment and go right upstairs." Still speaking softly, she added, "You want anything from the kitchen and it isn't too unreasonable, let me know at lunchtime. Maybe I can get it for you." She passed

58

Helena's chamber pot to the orderly, who emptied it into a large waste barrel on wheels.

"Coffee," Helena whispered, watching the unsanitary container being returned without first being rinsed. "Cream and sugar."

"I'll see what I can do." Another smile, and Millie locked Helena's door. Her humming faded as she continued down the hall.

Not knowing what happened to those who refused to eat, Helena choked down the gray matter in the bowl, wishing she had a little sugar. And butter. She hoped Millie hadn't handled other pots before delivering her breakfast, but she doubted it.

She set the bowl and cup near the door and lay face down on the cot, unable to shed a single tear regarding her appalling situation. How long would she be held a prisoner here? Weeks? Months? Years? Forever? Then her tears began in earnest.

Other than an occasional strange face peering in on her throughout the morning, she was left alone. At midday meal, Millie kept her word. She handed Helena a hot cup of coffee. Black. Helena didn't care so long as she had the coffee. She had never tasted anything so delicious in her life.

Later, as she used the chamber pot, she begged the Lord to keep everyone away from her door for a moment.

At six o'clock, Millie returned for the final time, handing Helena a pewter plate. There were a thin slice of unidentifiable meat, a cold biscuit, cold potatoes and peas, and more coffee. "I get off after supper, so I won't see you till morning." Lowering her voice, she added, "Remember, keep up your spirits. Don't let down for one second. They watch everybody real close. See you tomorrow." The orderly she had had with her that morning and noon was not present. Apparently Millie convinced someone he was no longer needed.

Helena was so grateful for Millie's kindness that she could barely keep from crying once again. To have a compassionate person within these horrid walls seemed to be a miracle.

A week passed before Mrs. A. brought Helena to Dr. Henry Holmes's office. By then she had learned to control her weeping and complaining. As dark as her thoughts had become, as much as she despised this godless place, she was determined to be whatever she needed to be, to do whatever she had to do to regain her freedom.

Priscilla continued to fully occupy her reflections; Helena desperately longed for her, but if by some magical trick she were returned home this instant, she was positive that Frederick would make certain the two of them never came near each other again. Her Priscilla was gone for all time.

"Mind your manners, now," Mrs. A. warned sharply.

Helena said nothing as Holmes waved her in. Rudely, he did not rise as she entered, keeping his eyes on the contents of a file folder — hers she hoped — as though she were not there.

He was a portly man with collar-length hair and great bushy sideburns the color of old faded corn. His beard was unkempt and yellowing like his hair. His jowls sagged and his eyelids were heavy with fat.

He continued reading as he set the folder on the desk and leaned forward. A bread crumb fell from his beard onto the file. Idly, he brushed at his beard and smoothed the front of his rumpled suit coat.

Disorderly stacks of files blanketed his desk. An ashtray overflowed with ashes and three different pipes. Pens lay scattered about. Behind his black leather chair were more folders piled against the wall. Muted light from a large, barred window behind him cast the room into gloomy shadows from the heavily overcast day. The rest of the dismal chamber contained four filing cabinets and a worn, black leather couch, plus the chair in which Helena now waited placed before the desk.

He finally looked up from the paperwork. "You're new here, I see. Came in last week Tuesday." Mrs. A. lingered behind Helena. Holmes looked at her. "Something else, Mrs. A.?"

"Just making sure she stays put, Doctor." She smiled at him, self-assured, confident of her position and status. "This one's a scrapper."

"That'll be all, Mrs. A." She nodded and left, leaving the door ajar.

"Close the door." She did, frowning her disapproval. Helena thought she heard him mutter, "Damned busybody."

Resting his elbows on his desk, he finally gave her his attention. She could feel his gaze pierce her inner being, penetrate her nostrils and mouth, slither through her ears and eyes. His probing scrutiny of her seemed to invade her skull, reach into her brain. She wanted to run, *run*! She clung to the sides of the seat to keep herself moored.

"Well, Miss McFarlane," he rumbled. As he leaned

back, the chair creaked in loud protest against his massive weight. "We can't just go around doing things and getting ourselves into situations in which we have no business being. It suggests a person's lack of self-control, and in your case, severe lack of control, including both physical as well as moral. Made worse, I might add, because you're of the female persuasion. I understand you fought with Mrs. Furant and Mrs. Bostson."

She'd been here seven days and all Dr. Holmes could think to ask first was about her struggles with two impossible women? And she hadn't even been successful at that. "That was a week ago, Dr. Holmes."

"I'm well aware of when it happened, Miss McFarlane."

She made no reply. The silence between them lengthened until she could stand it no longer. She asked, "When may I go home?"

"It'll be a while." He continued gaping at her, irritating and unnerving her. His watery blue eyes shifted restlessly in their deep, corpulent sockets, often straying to her bosom. She wanted to pluck each offending eyeball from his head, to grind it to pulp beneath her heel. He asked, "Why did you fight with the aides?"

"They were being brutal."

"And were you not being brutal in deliberately trying to hurt them?"

"They were both manhandling me, and so did two men. They . . . they . . ." She couldn't go on.

"You were scrapping with those who would help you, and by doing so you clearly demonstrated your lack of self-discipline and your unwillingness to adhere to the rules of this hospital." His tirade slowed as he said, "And you passionately kissed a woman." His eyes became heavy as he stared at her. His lips twitched as though he were fighting a smirk, making her feel dirty. What she and Priscilla had shared was *not* dirty. In an instant, she hated him as she had never hated anything or anyone before. Continuing, he asked, "Are you so disinclined to regain your correct state of mind through positive actions and a firm sense of management over your behavior?"

"Struggling against brutality is not a display of lack of control, Dr. Holmes. It is an attempt to save oneself from ridiculous and painful situations."

Holmes again leaned forward, resting his ham-like hands upon the desk's littered surface. "Miss McFarlane, you came here to be cured."

"I'm not ill."

"Your family believes you are."

"My family is wrong."

"And how is that?"

"I'm not insane. It's that simple."

"We'll talk again soon."

"When?"

"Soon."

Like that, she'd been dismissed.

He rang a small hand bell on his desk and picked up another file. Mrs. A. appeared before he had it opened. She came to Helena's side and waited for directions.

Rage bloated Helena's belly and mind. She thought she might attack Mrs. A. if the woman put so much as a single finger upon her. She glared at the nurse and said, "I can manage without your assistance."

She strode from the office and back to her room, where she threw herself upon her cot. Mrs. A. slammed the cell door before locking it, clearly a reprimand for Helena's momentary strike for independence.

At six, Millie brought her dinner. As she set the plate on the cot, Helena reached out and took her hand. The woman had been so kind and so good all week, even when Helena, in her worst moments, snapped needlessly at her. "Millie, I think you're a dear."

Millie carefully extracted her hand. "Why, thank you, Miss McFarlane. You're very nice yourself. I expect that soon you'll end up on the third floor."

Helena rose from the bed. Again taking Millie's hand and looking into her eyes, she asked, "Will you come to see me?"

Millie withdrew, backing away. "Miss McFarlane, you're a nice lady and such, but I don't think you ought to be grabbing at me like this."

"Why not, Millie? You're so good to me. So kind. I like it. Don't you? You are kind, you know."

Millie backed to the door. "No, ma'am, I don't like it. You be good now, you hear?"

Again the door was locked.

Helena sank to the cot. She could feel her face burning. Why did Millie act like that? Helena only wanted to hold her for a moment. She desperately needed to touch another human being.

She sat down and put her plate in her lap, eating without remembering how the food tasted or even what it was.

From her room, Helena could see the calendar behind the nurses' station. She had been here for six months. It might as well have been six years. In that time, she had received not a single word from her family, nor, of course, from Priscilla. As yet, she hadn't thought of a good way of killing herself, but nightly she entertained the idea. She would eventually find a solution. She had no intentions of spending the rest of her life in this lunatic asylum.

Two months ago, she was declared stable enough to walk the galley under the alert eyes of the staff but as yet, she hadn't been allowed to go to the dining hall. She paced for hours at a time, restless, and stared out her window with agonizing longing. Gray squirrels playfully darted here and there, digging through snow searching for last fall's hidden cache of nuts. Chickadees flitted about. Now and then a tufted titmouse or cardinal or blue jay would land in the nearby shrubbery. At one time Helena knew nothing of birds. Since coming here, she entertained herself daily by watching the perky feathered friends that clustered in the trees and high, thick bushes growing along the sidewalk.

Birds were brutal, she decided. They fought one another, drove the weaker ones away. Larger birds flew at the squirrels, though she didn't know why since the birds didn't seem to eat the acorns and chestnuts the rodents unearthed. Lovely things didn't necessarily indicate nicer things.

At one P.M., Mrs. A. came into her room like a great storm sweeping across the land. "Come with me. You're leaving."

Helena froze. "Why? Where?" Not the cage again. She couldn't take another night of that!

Mrs. A. stiffened; her eyebrows rose very high. Hastily, Helena collected the things she had gathered over the past half-year. Beside the clothing she wore, the same as when she had first arrived, she now owned a small bar of soap, a comb with missing teeth she had found on the galley floor and a brush delivered clandestinely by Millie during Helena's first week here. In five seconds she was ready to leave.

"Leave that trash and follow me," Mrs. A. growled. "And be quick about it."

Helena tossed the items onto the cot. She could barely walk as she followed Mrs. A.

Please, God, she prayed as her legs turned to jelly, I haven't done anything wrong. Don't let her put me in the cage again.

Chapter Eight

Helena was not taken to the horrifying cage. Instead, Mrs. A. led her briskly to the third floor. There were no chaotic goings-on here, no screaming, no begging for release.

They bypassed several dormitories before turning into one halfway down the galley. The room contained twenty beds, ten on either side of the room, each separated by a small stand. Several women sat around on cots, chatting with one another. There was vastly more light in this room than in Helena's cubicle and an immense sense of openness. She refrained from gasping at her new spacious surroundings.

"You'll stay here," Mrs. A. announced. "I did not recommend your being moved, but my opinion was discarded." She pointed to a bed farthest from the door. "You'll sleep at the end, there."

Helena was overcome with gratitude. "Oh, thank you, Mrs. A., thank you."

Mrs. A. stepped close to Helena, her eyes riveted on her. Helena felt the woman's murderous anger, her stark rage. Her gaze radiated venom. "I will be watching you, little Miss Helena. You carry yourself as though you think you're better than anyone else here. But you're not. You're no better than the worst of the lot. You step out of line once and it's back in the box for you." Her voice seethed. "And it won't be just one night, dearie."

Helena wanted to step back, but she dared not move a muscle. In a whisper, she said, "I won't cause any trouble, Mrs. A."

Mrs. A.'s mouth drew into a tight line. Her lips paled to a sickly white. "I doubt that. I doubt it one bit, so I'll be watching. Closely." She marched out the door, her back ramrod straight.

Helena staggered to her cot and collapsed facedown. The thin, worn mattress smelled from the urine, sweat and tears of bodies that had previously lain here over the years. As yet she had no sheet, blanket or pillow, but she hoped she would be given them before the day was over. Meanwhile, she could only lie there, weak from Mrs. A.'s threats and from relief at having been transferred. She cared not a tinker's damn that the mattress reeked.

She must have fallen asleep for a long time, for when she awoke the light was beginning to fade.

"It's suppertime if you'd care to go."

Helena rolled over to see her new neighbor.

"My name is Louisa. Welcome to Dormitory D."

Louisa's face was round as a pie plate. Her hair was piled neatly on top of her head and her brown eyes were calm and steady. She was a thin, short woman who emitted a sense of grace. She sat very straight upon her cot, her feet properly together, her hands folded and resting in her lap.

It had to be Louisa's steady voice and calm eyes that struck Helena so, inexplicably causing her to burst into tears and fling herself into the woman's arms.

Louisa rocked her while Helena sobbed. "I'm afraid, Louisa, I'm so afraid."

"Don't be, Helena." Louisa stroked her hair. "You'll be all right, now. You'll be fine."

"Mrs. A.," Helena said, choking between great gulps of air. "She's watching me."

"No, she isn't," Louisa whispered softly. "She's just a big bag of wind. Don't worry about her."

"She's going to send me back to the cage." Helena tried to sit up. She could not and Louisa didn't insist. The thought of the constraining cell drained her, and again she collapsed against Louisa's chest.

"She can't, Helena. Not unless you start a fight or look like you really are going crazy and begin to throw things around and tear them up."

Helena clutched Louisa's dress. "I would never do that. Never!"

"Then you have nothing to worry about. Besides, Mrs. A.'s authority extends only to the eating hall."

Helena drew herself upright as though she weighed thousands of pounds. Wiping her eyes with her sleeve, she asked, "That's all? Just in the hall and nowhere else?"

Louisa smiled, steadying Helena with an arm draped across her shoulder. "There, and Floor Two. She has no authority on this floor. She only delivers patients here, and she threatens every one of us with the same old line." Louisa lowered her voice and said, " 'It's the box for you, missy, and it won't be just one night this time, either.' "

"You sound exactly like her," Helena said sniffing and swiping at her dripping nose. She managed a slight smile.

Louisa nodded. "We can all ape her. Now, you forget all about her and let's go get something to eat."

"I don't think I can."

"Of course you can. You have friends waiting. They know you're coming." Louisa hauled Helena to her feet. "Those of us who live in this dormitory have known for a couple of days now."

Following along behind Louisa, Helena said, "But I didn't even know. How can this be?"

"Contacts," Louisa casually replied. "Friendly nurses. I've been sitting by your cot since right after you came upstairs."

"Why?"

"To make sure you had a friendly face to greet you when you woke up. To be sure you were all right. You snore in your sleep, do you know that?"

"No. I never used to."

"Well, we can all get used to that. There are others in the dormitory who snore, too. Quite loudly in some cases."

By the time they reached the table, Helena was only slightly afraid of Mrs. A.

Located on the first floor, the large dining hall was painted a dull white. Rows of long tables and benches filled the room. A spacious kitchen to the left operated at full steam. Clattering plateware and rattling pots and pans mingled with frequent shouts from an unseen, rumbling-voiced man barking out orders at great speed to the staff within.

The place was crammed with seventy or more women, some of whom Helena knew from the second floor. They were in all stages of sanity and dress, and most chatted energetically. Fifty or more ladies were already seated; another twenty-five waited in the serving line.

Herman stood guard at the door as Helena and Louisa joined the line. "Well, howdy, missy. They finally let you out, huh? Hey, Sadie," he said to the woman standing directly in front of Louisa. "Got some fresh blood for you."

"Fuck you, asshole." The woman named Sadie abruptly turned her back on him. Herman gestured to Mrs. A. some distance away. Apparently Mrs. A. thought Helena was not going to be a problem and she waved him off.

Before leaving, he chuckled saying, "Take good care of her now, Sadie, dearie, that being your talent and all."

"Fuck you," Sadie repeated acridly. She waited until Herman was gone before saying, "Are you Helena?"

Thoroughly disturbed by the use of such base language, Helena could only nod, moving a step closer to Louisa.

"Meet Sadie, Helena," Louisa said smiling.

Sadie spoke sympathetically. "I hope they weren't too rough on you."

"I spent a night in the cage." Helena spoke in a near whisper. Through it all, the cage had been her worst experience despite having had her hair ripped from her head. Thankfully, there was plenty of new growth and her jaw had healed up as well. She was glad no one at home could see how she looked. Especially Priscilla.

"I'm sorry." Sadie was exceedingly tall and thin. Within her pallid face, her eyes were ancient orbs smudged with large dark circles beneath, but Helena didn't think her to be older than twenty-five or -six. Her hair was neatly combed and held back with a piece of string. She wore a faded, shapeless gray dress, aged and frayed about the collar, cuffs and hem. Patches had replaced the elbows and several buttons were missing from the bosom. "They put me in there too, when I first got here. Been here a year so far and only been back in two other times."

"A year is a very long time." Surely, that wouldn't happen to her. Helena could not believe her family would allow her to remain in custody that long a time. A year was an eternity. And to have been in the cage *three* times.

"Come, dear. You need to eat." Louisa put her hand on Helena's shoulder. Helena gave silent thanks for having been delivered into the hands of these kind human beings. Sadie wasn't so frightening after all.

On long rectangular serving tables were stacks of spoons, pewter plates and metal water cups. Beyond that, large pans were heaped with cold corned beef, equally cold boiled potatoes and sliced bread. Behind the tables, male and female servers wearing heavily stained aprons over their uniforms stood poised holding large spoons. One of the servers scooped up corned beef and waited with annoyed impatience for Helena to pick up her plate.

Helena openly frowned at the food. "Is this our dinner?"

"That's it," Louisa answered. "Hope you like it." She smiled cynically.

"But . . . but it's not hot. It's nasty-looking. And there isn't even butter for the bread. And it smells awful."

Sadie chuckled. "You're probably just tired."

Helena's stomach recoiled. "I can't eat this, Sadie. I've never seen such awful board."

"You'll learn to like it just to keep from starving. So pick up your plate and spoon."

Helena continued gawking.

Someone snarled, "Come on, girl, move it. I ain't got all day."

Another growled, "Yeah, lady. Move your ass or get the hell outta line. I'm hungry even if you ain't."

Too frightened not to, Helena hurriedly picked up a plate. How could these women be hungry? How could anyone live on such offal?

Louisa nudged her along, whispering as they moved, "Let them serve you. If you don't eat, they'll force it into you."

Helena cast a panicky look at Sadie, whose nod confirmed Louisa's warning. Her voice trembled as she said, "I'll need a knife and fork as well." None had been laid out.

Nearby, an unkempt woman waiting in line laughed raucously, her mirth as brittle as thin ice. "Spoon's all you get here, sweetheart. You might be a danger to somebody with a knife and fork in your hand. I know I would be," she shouted to any who would listen. "I'd kill every sonofabitch in this goddamn place if I had a knife. Even a dull one."

She received the laughter she sought and a scolding from an orderly. "Shut your mouth, Natty, or you'll go hungry."

"Don't look at her, Helena," Louisa cautioned. "It'll bring you trouble."

"Louisa's right," Sadie agreed. "Natty ain't worth it."

Helena took their prudent advice, ignoring Natty's further angry mutterings. She bit her tongue and accepted the food being slopped onto her plate. Were she at home, she would likely be eating leg of lamb with mint jelly, creamy mashed potatoes loaded with butter and roast squash glazed with brown sugar. For dessert she would fill her stomach with dried-apple pie until she hurt.

"We'll eat over there." Sadie led them to the center of the dining hall. Helena followed with head bowed and shoulders slumped. Her family dog was better treated than this.

Louisa leaned close to her ear. "Come on, Helena. You must be strong." She gave Helena's sleeve a firm tug. "Otherwise you'll never get out of here." Helena and Sadie threaded their way between two rows of tables. "We always sit in the same area. I'll introduce you to the regulars who eat with us."

After meeting several other women, Helena spotted Mrs. A. looking right at her. Not looking so much as glaring. Helena glanced away and took a drink of tepid water.

As unobtrusively as possible, she studied other patients surrounding her. Most of them carried a similar look in their eyes — haunted, suspicious, restless and searching. Many wore blank, hopeless expressions. Some displayed tics around their cheeks, eyes, lips and chins. Very few smiled. Very few combed their hair, and many bore bruises upon their faces.

Almost without exception, the women were thin. Their dresses hung like sacks on them. Everywhere the reek of perspiration was offensively pungent. It gave Helena heart to see at least a few women looking as though they might have just stopped in to visit. They were neat and well groomed. They looked discouraged but not beaten. There had to be money in their backgrounds, she decided.

Helena lowered her face and closed her eyes. She must keep herself together. She must! She was not a part of these people, nor would she ever allow herself to become like them.

"All right, you asked for it, girl." Just down the line from where Helena sat came a sudden, protesting shout. A plate crashed noisily to the floor.

Helena jerked her head toward the commotion. Mrs. A., aided by a female orderly, pulled a patient from her seat and forced her to the floor. Helena's eyes grew wide with horror as she watched the poor woman hold up a protective hand against repeated slaps across her face.

Unblinking, Sadie said, "God, they're after Florena

again. When in hell is she gonna learn to quit fighting the sonsabitches? I keep telling her and telling her."

"Please stop," Florena begged. "I'll be good. I *swear* I'll be good. I'll eat. Let me up and I'll show you."

"You had your chance, missy." Mrs. A. sat across Florena's thighs. "For God's sake, Prudence, grab hold of her. Roberta, go get Martin. He's in the kitchen today. We need another plate of food out here. *Move it!*"

Roberta moved it. An orderly under Mrs. A.'s thumb, Helena gathered, and another big woman. Where did they all come from?

Prudence struggled to grasp Florena's failing arms as Martin hurried from the kitchen carrying a full plate of food.

Mrs. A. shouted to the dining room, the cords in her neck sticking out like steel cables, "Don't any of the rest of you move!" Some had begun to stand and sidle away. "Sit down," she roared again. Wild-eyed and agitated, they sat.

Sadie did not. "Now, this, Helena, is worth my time." She rose defiantly, then moved purposefully toward the ruckus.

Helena's eyes were glued to Sadie's back.

By now Mrs. A. and Prudence had fully restrained Florena. Martin quickly knelt beside her.

"Feed her, Martin. Now!" Mrs. A. glared at him as he tried to grab hold of Florena's rolling, bobbing head.

Florena was stubborn and strong, dodging his

76

hand as long as she could until he managed to force her jaw open the same way he had Helena's.

The scuffling group had been too busy to notice Sadie until she stood beside them. She reached out and yanked away Martin's hand causing Florena to cry out as his fingers were ripped away. With lightning speed, he backhanded Sadie's shins, staggering her from the blow. He moved quickly, not unlike a large snake striking his enemy, as he leaped up and grabbed her. In no time, he had her arms pinned behind her thin body, his own pressing hard against her back.

"Put her in the cage where she'll cool off," Mrs. A. ordered. "And send Tom here to finish this mess. Be quick about it."

"Yes, ma'am."

Helena started to leave the table. She wanted to run from here. She could flee like a bird, escape, never come back.

Louisa grabbed her arm. Sharply, she whispered, "No! Just keep eating." Louisa held her until Helena put a spoonful of food in her mouth, but she could not tear her attention away from the ruckus going on so near her. Her heart pounded as Sadie, fighting and screaming damning epithets, was dragged away.

A rush of lightheadedness attacked her and she began to slump. Louisa put an arm around her waist, steadying her until she could lift her head again. Other patients were either whispering or whimpering.

There was no grappling this time. Tom was very efficient, reopening Florena's jaw, shoving in a wedge and spooning corned beef into her mouth.

Florena began to choke. Tom struck her sharply on her back until she stopped, then forced more food down her. Again she coughed and choked and was smacked until she recovered enough to swallow another spoonful.

In time, she ate everything on the plate, then was roughly reseated at the table. Prudence and Tom moved off to other areas of the room. "Get the idea, Florena?" Mrs. A.'s face was beet red; sweat drenched her uniform.

Florena was quiet now. She was given yet another plate of food. Slowly, mechanically, she lifted her spoon eating one tiny bite at a time. Mrs. A. stood like a granite pillar directly behind her, watching, watching, watching while the room settled down.

Mrs. A. pressed a hand to her lower back. "All right, everybody. Back to your quarters."

Protests erupted throughout the room. Many hadn't finished their dinner.

"You should have been paying attention to your own business," Mrs. A. yelled. "Then you would have had plenty of time. It's your own stupid fault."

There was a collective moan throughout the hall. Spoons and cups rapped against plates; benches screeched as they were pushed back. Women talked loudly over the noise while stuffing food into their mouths as they lined up to clean their dinnerware and stack everything on a nearby table.

Back in Dormitory D, Helena's meager belongings and bedding had been left on her cot. She made the bed and put her possessions on her stand before lying down. The few bites of food she had managed to get down lay like lead in her stomach.

She fell asleep and dreamed of women being beaten, of her being without a stitch of clothing on and desperately trying to cover her nakedness with just a small towel and failing. More women now, dying by drowning, dying by suffocation in the cage.

She whimpered and thrashed and cried throughout the night, and throughout the night, Louisa sat beside her, cooling Helena's fevered brow with a damp cloth, moving back to her cot and feigning sleep when the orderlies passed through to check the patients. When they left, she arose again to tend Helena, who wept.

Chapter Nine
Laurie, 1960

It was ten when Eveleen poked her head into her grandmother's room. She carried a heavily scrolled silver tray. On it were ham sandwiches, two mugs and a pot of strong, aromatic coffee. "Still pontificating, huh, Grandma? Thought you two might like something to eat. Got dill pickles, too. Grandma, I brought you a hot bowl of Cream of Wheat, just like you like it. Plenty of maple syrup and cream." Ev carefully set the tray on the bed. "Black coffee, right, Laurie?" Ev glanced at her, but she was still dazed, sitting stock-still, staring wide-eyed at the floor. "She okay, Grandma?" She busily fluffed her grandmother's pillows.

"She will be," Grandma said, chuckling. "I'll start with the coffee."

Laurie reached for a sandwich and mindlessly bit into it.

"Please, Grandma," Ev pleaded. "No coffee. You know it gives you heartburn and terrible gas."

"Coffee. And blacker than hell." Grandma's fixed stare was stone cold. "You got two cups there."

"I was hoping you'd pass it up this time."

"Foolish girl. What's a cup of coffee gonna do to me at my age?"

Eveleen placed a brimming cup on the stand. She smiled through tears not yet boiling over but threatening to at any moment. Leaving the tray behind, she quietly closed the door as she left.

Laurie, still immersed in the gripping story of Helena's life, didn't feel that she was completely there, sitting in Grandma's room, in her house, in this century. She blinked hard several times to disengage herself from the bothersome sensation, somehow aware that something important had just occurred between Ev and Grandma.

"I think she feels bad that you scolded her, Grandma."

"Nonsense."

"She's crying."

"She wasn't scolded, dear. Not even flustered. Now don't you worry about it."

"Are you sure?" Laurie questioned lightly. She began to rise. "I'll get her for you. You two can talk things —"

"No need. Her feelings ain't a bit hurt. Now, where was I?"

Yes, Laurie believed, Ev was hurt, and this cranky, demanding old woman brushed off the incident as though it didn't matter that she had just humiliated her great-great-granddaughter in front of her best friend. She felt a twinge of anger toward the old woman. Laurie's loyalty lay first and always with Eveleen.

"You're not listening, Laurie, dear." Grandma was patting her hand.

No, Laurie hadn't been listening. She didn't want to listen. She wanted to go to bed and not wake up until tomorrow — late. Fatigue was swiftly consuming the last of her momentum. As politely as possible, she said, "We've been talking for a long time, Grandma. Wouldn't you like to get some sleep now?" She looked pointedly at her watch.

"No, take another look at that drawing."

Sighing and responding like a well-trained dog, Laurie did as she was bidden. She was incapable of arguing with Grandma. "And pass me a pickle. Always did love pickles. Makes you pucker right up, don't they? And look there," she said as she pointed, "at that woman standing next to Helena, there."

Guiltily, Laurie gave the crone a pickle. Grandma noisily and thoughtfully sucked on it for a while, then put it aside.

Her narrative of Helena McFarlane had become so real, so alive, that to regard the others frozen in time alongside this sad and broken-hearted lady seemed a near act of desertion.

"Grandma," she said, standing as a new surge of anger flowed through her. She had to get out of there for a while. "I need to go to the bathroom and I need to say hello to Ev. I haven't had a real chance to do that yet, and I feel rather bad about it."

"Go to the bathroom and then come straight back. My Eveleen can wait."

"No, she can't, Grandma. *I* can't wait. *I* need to see her."

Grandma's lips tightened, then relaxed. Unsmiling, she said, "All right, then, go on. You should say a proper hello, I suppose. But don't be long. I ain't got all night."

Laurie patted the woman's aged hand and moved to the door. "I'll be back in fifteen minutes."

"Promise?"

"I promise."

She found Ev on the porch, tucked in a rocker, her feet drawn beneath her. In the last of the evening's fading light, she softly hummed a tune.

Laurie discreetly cleared her throat, not wanting to startle her. Ev looked toward the door, then quickly turned away. Tears glazed her cheeks.

Laurie's eyes narrowed with concern as she moved to kneel beside Ev. "Grandma's very sick, isn't she? Is she . . ." Laurie couldn't bring herself to complete her thought.

"Yes, she's going to die. Very soon."

"Like . . . in weeks, months . . . days?" Laurie put her hand over Ev's.

"That depends on a lot of things, right now."

"Like what? What does it depend on?"

Ev dropped her eyes.

"I'm awfully sorry, Ev. I know how you love her."

"She's been my primary female support since Mom died." She paused, then said, "Twelve years. Seems like yesterday."

For three months following her mother's death, Ev had cried. Frequently. And each time Laurie had held her. "Is there someone who could help you through this, Ev? Someone special, a boyfri —"

Ev scoffed angrily, pushing aside Laurie's hand. She left the rocker and stepped off the porch. Staring into the darkness, she said, "I can handle it, Laurie."

Laurie rose and took a step toward her. "I held you after your mom died, Ev. I can certainly do the same now."

Ev faced her. The light from the living room lamps created delicate shadows and highlights upon her face. "And then what, Laurie? In a month you'll be gone. I can't see myself becoming attached to you like that ever again."

Ev's words immobilized Laurie, actually stunned her. She herself felt as close as ever to Ev. She had no idea that Ev had distanced herself from Laurie over the years. To gain a little time to adjust to her injured feelings, she took the opportunity to seat herself. She said, "All right, Ev. But I do care how you feel."

Impatiently, Ev brushed back some strands of hair that a warm, soft breeze had blown across her eyes. "Oh, shut up, Laurie. I'm hurting, that's all. God, I would think you'd see that right away, especially after all the years we've known each other. Especially *this* kind of pain."

"What kind?" Laurie said more caustically than she meant to. "You're losing a very, very close and loving relative. You're grieving terribly. I do understand."

Ev returned to her rocker, angrily throwing herself onto the seat. It skidded backward several inches from the force of her weight. "Oh, God, Laurie. We never quarrel. We never have. Let's just drop it, shall we, and talk about something else? Something light."

"Well, let me see," Laurie said cheerfully, not feeling cheerful at all. She drew her rocker next to Laurie's and gave her friend a light punch on the arm. "Your grannie weaves an enchanting spell. I almost didn't know where I was when you came into the room. Helena must have been quite a woman."

Ev chuckled, nodding. "I think so. She knew how to love, all right."

"Are you serious? She was a . . . a queer."

"She knew how to love."

Embarrassed, but too curious not to, Laurie had to ask. "And, uh, how was that?" Other than what Grandma had just revealed she had no clear idea of what women did in bed.

"Completely and unconditionally."

It was not what Laurie expected to hear, but she didn't know how to press the issue. "But she was a queer. What a weird thing to be."

Ev's rocker stilled. "How so?"

"Well." Laurie's face warmed further. She was grateful that the night was now full upon them. "I can't imagine going to bed with somebody of the same sex, can you?" That might get her some information.

Ev shrugged. "I don't know. Might depend on the person."

"Oh, now, seriously, Ev." Laurie laughed nervously. "You can actually *imagine* such a thing happening to you after all the men you've slept with?"

Ev looked questioningly at Laurie. "Where'd you get that idea?"

"Just from hearing about all the dates you've had, the things you told me."

"I never told you who I slept with, or, I might add, how many times."

"Well, I sure gathered from our midnight chats that it was often enough."

Ev laughed. "Okay, think what you want. It sounds good to me."

"So did you sleep with lots of men?"

"You don't know, do you?"

"No, that's why I'm asking."

Both rockers were moving at their fastest speeds now, creaking in concert with each other, causing them to inch backward until they were up against the house.

"These things travel like lightning," Laurie said, returning her chair to the edge of the porch. She resettled herself and began rocking again. "You know, I don't know why Grandma told me such an elaborate story about a queer friend of hers from way the hell back when."

"Can't you just listen and enjoy the story?" Ev, too, had repositioned her rocker.

"I suppose. But why tell me? I don't know anything about those kinds of people."

"Maybe there's a lesson to be learned in there somewhere."

Laurie looked at Ev's dark form, sensing a new tension growing between them. "Are you pissed at me personally about something, Ev? You've been a little strange since I got here, and frankly, I'm becoming uncomfortable with it."

Ev sighed tiredly. "No." She gazed into the night. "Listen to those coyotes howl. They are so free. Their life is so hard, but they're so incredibly free."

"What makes them free if their lives are that difficult?" Laurie fought a growing irritation toward Ev.

After a long pause, Ev replied. "They're free from choice."

"You need a drink, girl."

Ev didn't respond.

Laurie rose heavily. "I've got to go back to Grandma. Why don't you join us?"

Ev shook her head.

"Oh, come on, Eveleen."

"I've heard the stories before."

"Well, then come and hear them again. At least we'll be in the same room together, and I could do with that. Good Lord, Ev, I haven't seen you in a whole damn long year."

"You go, Laurie. The stories are for you."

"Bull. Come on, Ev. Grandma won't care."

"The stories are for you. They're a gift from Grandma. A gift for you."

Laurie sighed. "I don't understand you, but I still

love you, although right now, I'd have to sift through all that mulishness of yours to see just why. I'll see you later." The door squeaked as she pulled it open.

"Laurie?"

Laurie looked back at her aching friend. "Yes?"

"Remember that time in college when I disappeared for several weeks without telling you why?"

"I remember."

"Why do you think I was gone?"

Laurie closed the door and returned to kneel before Ev, resting her hands on her friend's thighs. Ev's jeans smelled of dust and horse sweat. Her legs, tightly encased within, felt rock-hard. "You are so strong."

Ev inhaled deeply as she placed her hands over Laurie's, caressing them with the balls of her thumbs. Insects filled the night with intri- cate, melodious hymns.

"What did you think back then, Laurie?" Ev's voice had dropped to a whisper.

"I thought you had had an abortion and that . . . it hadn't gone well. I thought you were recovering from it."

"You're dead wrong, Laurie, but I forgive you."

Forgive her? For what? What had she done that she would need Ev's forgiveness? Laurie had finally had it with Ev's indecipherable statements. And there were still more of Grandma's chronicles to face about who knew what next. Probably another queer story. That's all she needed to hear just before going to bed. She'd be dreaming she'd be attacked by one of them. That is, if she ever got to bed. God, she was tired. Maybe more tired than Grandma, at the moment. She left Ev rocking in silence.

Pausing at Grandma's door, she collected her wits about her.

"Come in here, gal. You're later than fifteen minutes."

Laurie took the chair, grabbed her mug and swallowed. She relied on the coffee's painfully hot temperature to jog her alert and its strong caffeine to keep her awake. She apologized for her tardiness as she was handed the framed drawing.

"This here's Louisa S. Fairweather, the one who helped Helena in the crazy house," Grandma pronounced, pointing with a shaky hand at the woman standing beside Helena.

Laurie's seething thoughts were: *Grandma, I really don't give a damn.*

Chapter Ten
Louisa, 1874

"Open up, Louisa, immediately!" So violent was the knock upon her door that the unexpected noise jarred her to her teeth.

Dear God in heaven, William was terribly furious with her again, as he had been for a number of weeks now.

"I'm not finished bathing, dear," the short, stocky woman called out pleasantly, an attempt to soothe him. "I'll hurry —"

"Immediately," he roared through their bedroom door.

She had never heard him so angry before. "Yes, dear." She forced herself to speak sweetly as fear began to rapidly build within her.

She sprang from the galvanized tub, painfully banging her knee against its edge. No one, not even William, had ever been allowed to see her fully unclothed. Thank goodness she had thought to bolt the door. Dripping wet, she scrambled for her petti-coat, hastily pulling it on.

An ax shattered part of the door and she leaped in terror. "William, my God, what is happening out there?"

"I'm warning you, Louisa, let us in. Now!"

Us? Were the children here?

The blade struck again as she yanked a dress over her head and scrambled onto the bed. She pulled the goosedown covers to her chin as the door burst open, slamming against the wall.

William charged into the room, a double-bladed ax in his hand. He was not a tall man, yet his normal bearing made him appear so, with his black hair and thick beard and mustache barely touched with silver. In the chapel, his voice boomed across his flock as he preached Sunday sermon.

Louisa Susanne Fairweather, the good wife of Reverend William Horatio Alexander Fairweather, shrieked at him, "What is the meaning of this, William? Leave this room immediately." Louisa could feel her usually serene, maternal features tense. She was pleased with her looks. Her full face was round, her blue eyes merry, and her nose turned up at the tip. She was always ready to break into a smile or chuckle. She was short and plump, giving her, some said, a childlike appearance. At gatherings following each Sunday's service, people flocked to her as much as they did to her husband. She always had a kind word for them or laughed at something funny they said or sounded sympathetic when things weren't going well.

Now, she could tell, her face had become twisted in terror as she gazed at William's ax. Coldly he said, "Check her."

Immediately, a sheriff entered whom she didn't recognize, his badge looming larger than the bright morning sun, and Doctors Hiram X. Thurmond and James Patters Bookerton, both devout and active members of her husband's Presbyterian church. Their faces were impossible to read.

"I ask you again, sirs, how *dare* you enter a lady's chamber?" Her body tightened and she held her breath. The sheriff circled to the far side of the bed. Louisa tracked him while still attempting to keep both the doctors and William within view. "Why are you *here*?" The men slowly advanced upon her.

Condescendingly, Dr. Bookerton moved to the bedside, saying, "Now, now, Mrs. Fairweather, we're here to help you." His bulk, wrapped in a too-tight, rumpled brown wool suit, dwarfed her as he moved ever nearer the bedside. He spoke through a drooping dark red mustache. His great thatch of red hair, always a source of amusement to Louisa, now looked like Hades' flames leaping wildly from the devil's own skull.

"Help me with what? I need no help here. Please leave this room instantly." Her voice neared hysteria.

Dr. Thurmond knelt upon the bed, snatching away

the blanket. Before she knew it, he had seized her wrist in an iron grip.

Tears began coursing down her cheeks, and her face distorted in dread as she fought his powerful grasp. With his free hand he took her pulse. "Her heart is beating wildly," he said, grunting with the effort of holding her arm still. "Please verify, Dr. Bookerton, if you will."

Bookerton, a thin man with balding head, had moved to the bed's opposite side. "No!" She sobbed, attempting to twist away from both doctors tightly holding her arms. Shame saturated her at being so randomly handled by others as William stood by and watched. How could he not help her? How could these men of medicine, men she had known for years, treat her in such a base manner? They had delivered her three children, had sat at her table giving thanks, worshiped in William's church. A scream clawed at her throat for release.

Simultaneously, the doctors released her and quickly removed themselves from the bed. She again drew the covers, this time up to her eyes. She had been violated! *Violated!*

"Do you both concur?" Fairweather asked the physicians. His fierce expression defied them to challenge him; he still carried the ax in his hand.

Each nodded his agreement as Dr. Thurmond announced in a grave voice, "We do, indeed. Your wife's pulse races wildly through her veins."

"Of *course* my blood races through my veins," Louisa cried. "How do you expect it to do anything less under such terrifying and idiotic conditions? Leave me and I assure you it will return to normal."

"Sad it is to say," Thurmond continued, "I'm

93

afraid that we must declare your wife..." He looked upon Louisa with woeful eyes, the bags beneath them appearing to carry the weight of ten years' lack of sleep. He coughed politely once. ". . . hopelessly insane, Reverend Fairweather. I'm sorry."

"Insane, sir? You lie!" She dropped her protective covers and ran to her husband. "William, why are you doing this? *Why?*" She clung to him, frantically, desperately, in mortal fear for her life.

"Sheriff, the law states that . . ." Her husband pulled what appeared to be a legal document from his coat pocket. ". . . a man may place his wife in an insane asylum without evidence of insanity. This law was passed," he said knowledgeably, "February fifteenth, eighteen fifty-one. I am not needlessly placing my wife in the asylum. You see that I've carefully given her every consideration by bringing in two learned doctors who have verified my suspicions. Now, please . . ." At last he set aside the ax.

With a wave of his hand, he indicated she was to be removed from the room. He ignored her pleadings and racking sobs, her battering his chest with her fists, her grasping his abundant beard with both hands, beseeching him to *look — at — her.*

"Why?" She clenched his sleeve as he started for the door.

Turning on her, he roared, "Let go of me, you damnable woman. You have no place in my house or in my bed. You are unfit as a wife and mother." His eyes filled with rage. "Put on your shoes. *Now!*" He turned to the others. "Sheriff, you heard these doctors state that my wife is insane. Now, take her away from here, from this God-fearing family and home. But do it gently, sirs. I warn you."

Loudly, briskly, the sheriff called, "In here, gentlemen."

Coarsely dressed and smelling heavily of manure and stale ale, two large men, both of whom were unfamiliar to her, entered the bedroom. Louisa moved closer to William, wondering where on God's earth he had collected these strangers. How long had he been planning this dastardly move?

"Come now, Mrs. Fairweather. Just let us walk you downstairs." One of the men moved behind her.

"I'm not going anywhere with you," she hissed. "Remove yourselves from this sleeping room straight away. All of you."

The chamber had filled with stalking hunters. She, warily watching every man, felt trapped, condemned, doomed by the harsh realization that William was not going to change his mind, was not going to help her at all. It was a horrible blow. For twenty-four years, her devoted husband had been her strength, her guide, her life.

"William," she begged. "Please, think of our children, our marriage . . . Of me . . ."

"Women who think for themselves cause undue trouble for their husbands and their families. For several months you have openly disagreed with my teachings. St. Paul knew exactly what he was talking about when he wrote to the Corinthians. He certainly understood women and their weak brains and inability to function as full-thinking human beings. And he certainly had you in mind. Women have their place and you have willfully stepped out of yours. You have caused considerable unrest in my congregation amongst the women and have undone years of work with my youth. Your daughter and sons all agree with me."

"All? *All?* My children, my babies agree with you? How could they? *Why* would they? I've spoken only of women taking their equal right alongside their hus-bands and sons and of giving thought to other avenues of religion. Nothing more. How could they possibly disagree with that?"

"I convinced them." He spoke with no emotion, looking unwaveringly into her eyes. "They see the light now."

"Not Molly. Not my dear, sweet little Molly. She wouldn't. She *couldn't*." Her sobs began anew.

"For God's sake, Louisa, get hold of yourself. Molly is twenty-four years old. You are a grand-mother of three."

She was sure she was having a dreadful night-mare. At any moment she would wake up, and there to hold and soothe her would be William, strong William, believable William with whom she had shared so many good years.

"Gentlemen, *now!*" He watched impassively as those selected to escort his wife approached her. Their size, their strength, their grasp overwhelmed her as they easily lifted and carried her through the door toward the stairs. As they began their descent, she fought as though demons were handling her.

Having preceded them, Fairweather and the doctors waited at the landing, the sheriff following the struggling bearers of Mrs. Fairweather. Several times, all three nearly tottered as she brutally skirmished with them and clawed at their faces.

"Grab her, for God's sake," Fairweather shouted at them.

The men endured scratches and bites, kicking feet and flailing arms. Louisa howled like a wild thing caught in an animal trap. "My babies, what about my babies? My little ones." Frantically, she searched for Molly, her head swiveling as she was carried through the front door. Molly was coming over this morning. She was due now. She would save her.

She saw none of her children at all.

On the porch William ordered, "Put her in the buggy, gentlemen."

Carefully, they placed the screaming, battling woman on the leather-upholstered seat. They both breathed deeply when she had been deposited and wiped away sweat and blood from scratches and bites on their faces. The waiting driver grabbed her and held her fast.

"*Don't you touch me,*" she shrieked. She fought frantically, trying to dismount the seat, but the driver roughly pulled her down again.

"Now, sit, Missus, and I won't be having to get hard with you. You a lady of breeding acting such." His words dumbfounded her as she took in this latest tormentor. Like those who had just clapped her onto the buggy, he too was a man unknown to her and similarly dressed to those who had placed her here. He too had had a nip or two.

Grievously, she charged, "Does drink give you the strength to manhandle a lady of breeding, driver?" She swung her arm in a wide arc. "Is this how you, all of you so-called gentlemen, treat a misjudged woman? A wife of twenty-four years and a mother and grandmother? Do you do it by imbibing? Is this how you acquire your courage, how you win your wars and discipline your wives and your children? Dear God, deliver me from men such as these!"

Taken aback by such a lengthy and unexpected speech, the driver was clearly unprepared for her renewed lunge toward freedom. She was halfway out of the seat before he could catch her and uncompromisingly thump her down. "Don't act like that, ma'am. You're to ride with me. Now see that you do it proper." He put a firm arm around her waist.

Her hair and clothing had fallen into total disarray and her eyes felt bloodshot and raw from crying so hard. One sleeve of her blouse had been badly torn. William tried to throw her spring cloak over her shoulders but she thrust it away. "I don't need a cloak, William. I need you. Why are you doing this to me?"

"We've been through this already, Louisa," he said, ignoring her rejection of his parsimonious kindness.

"Dr. Thurmond, Dr. Bookerton, I beg of you. Please don't let William send me away. I'm not insane. I'm not, I'm *not*!" Her voice crescendoed to a high wail, inordinately audible in the still morning air.

Several neighbors had gathered, witness to the catastrophic scene taking place in front of the reverend's small two-story home shaded beneath tall elm trees. Some men verbally defied what was happening, others quietly watched. Women wrung their hands in helplessness as tears flowed unchecked down their cheeks. A few local dogs were drawn to the growing assembly by the unusual commotion. Their loud piercing barks each time Louisa screamed helplessly to her neighbors and to her husband added to the increasing confusion.

"What's to become of my children?" she pleaded with any who would look at her. "They need their mother."

Lanky John Schmidt, who was the Fairweathers' nearest neigh- bor, walked up to William and spoke in his quiet way, "Let 'er be, Reverend. She's a fine woman." His ice- blue eyes glanced sympathetically in her direction.

"You're making a sorrowful mistake, Reverend," said another of Fairweather's neighbors.

"You'll not see me in your church anymore," another man called.

"The devil's in you, man," a woman bravely shouted.

The reverend ignored them all. To interfere with another man's business could land a body in jail. No one was fully willing to risk that.

The single-horse rig rumbled away.

At this time of year the morning air was crisp and clean. Each leaf on every tree stood out in sharp relief. Rhododendrons would soon blossom, wild columbines were already making their presence known, and violets exhibited their proud purple. Those that Louisa had transplanted from a field to the back yard last fall were due to bloom any day now. The whole lovely town of Woburn, Massachusetts, was bursting with new life. She couldn't leave it. She couldn't!

Her caterwauling continued as the buggy moved

along at a brisk clip. The driver continued to hold her.

"William," she cried out. "Who will take care of my babies? My little ones. William, *William,* don't do this to our children. They need their mother."

She strained to look back over her shoulder. William had already gone back into the house, but her good neighbors still remained, all gaping at her as the buggy continued on.

Chapter Eleven

Louisa would forevermore consider June 3, 1874, equally as infamous as the day Mr. Lincoln was killed back on April 14, 1865. How could people be so very, very cruel to one another?

She was weak as a kitten from having been so crudely treated by strange men and *deserted* by her husband before being thrust into the hands of the complete stranger beside her. She was sure he wouldn't hesitate to strike her if she misbehaved.

She brooded in stony silence, lost in complete despair as the buggy bounced along for hours. Her driver offered no name and she didn't ask. She did not want his identity instilled within her memory. She wished him to become a nameless, faceless being she would one day no longer remember.

One brief stop was made while she relieved herself. "Stay close enough for me to hear you, ma'am," the driver warned, "or I'll be coming after you."

Behind thick bushes, shame consumed her as she exposed her buttocks to the earth. She feared the man would leap upon her, and in her haste to complete her task, she peed on her shoe and the hem of her dress. Humiliated beyond measure, she returned to the buggy vastly consoled to see that he apparently hadn't moved. She climbed aboard and this time he did not hold her. They had traveled too far to make it possible for her to escape.

Several hours later they arrived in Burlington, going straight to the train station. Taking her firmly by the arm, the driver steered her to a ticket window. "Two second-class tickets to Lowell, Massachusetts."

Never before had she traveled this far from home, much less accompanied by a strange man. His words evoked renewed terror within her, and her knees threatened to give way. "I must sit," she whispered. "I'm ill." She was sure she was going to swoon, or perhaps her heart would stop beating altogether.

"You're all right," he snapped, giving her arm a yank. "Pull yourself together."

Somehow she did, rather than endure the curious onlookers glancing their way. He snatched up the tickets and they boarded the train, Louisa conducting herself with an iron will.

Her clothing was in a shameful state, her hair in disarray, her face and hands soiled. Yes, she thought, I look like one ready for an insane asylum.

But I'm not, she wanted to scream. I'm not. I'm a mother of three, a loving wife, a good woman.

She didn't scream. She obeyed. Behaving genteelly could lead the doctors to realize instantly that she was perfectly normal and release her right away. All they had to do was speak with her. Surely they would discern that she was in no way mentally impeded.

The driver positioned her between the window and himself. He would escort her all the way there. But why not William, or one of her sons, Brett or David? Why this utter stranger? She doubted that any of her children knew what had truly happened, that she had been taken away against her will and was about to be placed in a lunatic asylum.

She shrank from her custodian's side, asking, "Whose wife will you next tear from her family, driver?"

"Shut your yap," he snarled in a whisper.

"Who?"

As though putting a hand on his dear wife, he took hers in his own and smiled. Squeezing slowly, he quietly repeated, "Shut your yap." Sharp pain blinded her as her fingers were crushed together. She started to scream just as he released her. His eyes became vicious glints in the late-afternoon light. "I can have you stowed in the baggage car, ma'am. It's nothing to me. I get paid either way. You behave and you can have a nice comfortable ride. Anything else, you become baggage."

She turned away, absently staring out the window,

massaging her hand, fighting the wrenching pain still lingering there. She would not cry. She would *not*. She would calm herself. Aggravating him accomplished nothing. She prayed for strength as the train's clicking wheels carried her ever farther from her home.

Chapter Twelve
Laurie, 1960

Laurie yawned widely. The bedside clock may have read midnight, but Grandma's eyes were still as bright as a rising morning sun. Did the woman never tire? "Mind if I move around a bit, Grandma?" She rose, stretching like a feline.

"You look like a good strong woman, Laurie, dear." Grandma reached for her coffee and took a hefty swallow.

"I exercise a lot at the YWCA near where I

work." Laurie could feel her muscles crying to unwind.

"That sitting behind a desk all day long can get tiresome I expect. Not like real work."

"Oh, it's real enough," Laurie answered defensively, sitting down again, knowing that she would not escape Grandma so easily this time. "I get worn out just trying to keep everybody happy around the place. That's exercise enough right there."

"But not work kind of work, though."

"I think it is."

"Don't you ever want to just get out there and push your body real hard?"

"Sure, and I do. At the YWCA three times a week."

"Doing what?" Grandma's eyebrows rose in obvious skepticism.

"I swim and play tennis with Joe. And I do sit-ups. Fifty or sixty of them each night before I go to bed."

"Good gosh, girl. What for?"

"To keep my stomach muscles strong. Keep my belly flat."

Grandma collapsed in laughter. Tears ran down her cheeks and her toothless mouth folded inward. "If that don't beat all. Seems like all you'd wanna do is get in bed at the end of a long day and stretch out comfortable." She continued cackling with mirth.

"I'm proud of my sit-ups," Laurie retorted. And of her strength and her flat tummy.

"All right, then," Grandma said, chuckling as she composed herself. "Fill up my cup there, will you, and let's get on with my stories."

"I need to pee."

"Later."

"Grandma," Laurie said in a pleading voice.

Grandma paused for a long time as she studied Laurie. "You do look a bit tired."

"I am, Grandma. I'm very, very tired."

"I want to tell you about Honora Unsworth."

"What about Honora Unsworth?" Laurie dropped her head to her hands and scooped up her long hair, pushing it away from her face. She tilted her head back, letting go of the thick mane, and kneaded her tired neck muscles. "Can she go with me to the bathroom? If I promise not to leave you longer than a few minutes, can Honora and I go pee?" Laurie grinned tiredly. She could barely sit upright.

Grandma closed her eyes. "You need to know about Honora, Laurie. You really do."

Laurie patted Grandma's hand. "I know I do, Grandma." But she had no idea why. "When did you meet all these people?" she asked.

"Oh, honey, except for Henry, I never knew any of them personally. I only just read about them in letters that Helena sent me."

And just who the hell was Henry?

"Still got 'em all, too. Right there in my bureau and tied with a blue ribbon, they are. My favorite color."

"Oh." Laurie propped her elbows on her knees and rested her head in her hands. "I thought these people were once personal friends of yours."

"They are, child, they are, and I love each and every one of them like they was my own kin. But I never knew but one of them."

Which one? Laurie wondered, but was too damned tired to ask. She felt her brain slithering around within her skull as she stood up, fiercely rubbing her eyes with balled fists. "I have to go pee." She had drunk far too much coffee.

"Laurie, sit down!" Grandma struggled to rise.

"Grandma, you can chase me down the hall if you wish, but I'm going to the bathroom. Would you like me to call Ev and have her help you, too?"

"Nope, use a catheter now."

Laurie hadn't noticed. She wondered when the old lady had been hooked up to that cumbersome thing. "Then I'll be back shortly, and if you're still awake, we'll talk. If not, morning is soon enough." She left, ignoring Grandma's noisy demands that she return right now.

She sank gratefully onto the toilet seat and leaned on her knees. She sat for several gratifying minutes before washing her hands and seeking out Ev, but Ev had gone to bed.

Laurie wondered if she should wake her or not. In the end, she decided to and quietly opened Ev's door.

Ev stirred, muttering sleepily, "That you, Laurie? Come on in. Did Grandma finally quit talking?"

Laurie sat on the edge of the bed. "Not yet. I had to go to the bathroom so badly that I just up and left. I couldn't wait anymore."

"She'll be fine." Ev yawned and sighed. "Lie down beside me for a while."

"There's not much room."

Ev moved over, pulling back the blanket, then patted the sheet. "Now there is."

"For a minute." Laurie lay straight out, her hands at her sides, not touching Ev. She was uncomfortable and self-conscious. "I'm not really relaxing, Ev. I should go to my own room."

Ev rolled next to Laurie and threw an arm and a leg across Laurie's body. "Nah, you'll relax in a minute. Just think about lying next to Joe."

Laurie continued resting, if she could call it that. Tension was palpable throughout her body as Ev snuggled even closer, saying in a sleepy voice, "You're a lot like holding a bale of hay. Soft, but packaged so tightly that there's only hard spots to you. Relax."

"I'm lying next to a woman with her arm around me and her leg locking mine together. How do you expect me to relax?"

"Make believe I'm Joe."

"You don't smell like Joe."

"How's Joe smell?"

"I don't know. Kind of sweaty at the end of the day. Like paint. Like . . . a man smells."

"I didn't shower this evening," Ev mumbled, her mouth burrowed against Laurie's hair. "I should smell something like that."

Laurie concentrated on Ev's body. She did smell of sweat and horses and grease from supper odors. "You smell like this ranch."

"You like the ranch?"

"I love the ranch."

"And I love your smell. I don't think you've changed your perfume once in all the years I've known you."

Ev's breath was warm and heavy, tickling Laurie's neck. As she reached up to scratch, Ev grasped her hand, bringing both to rest upon Laurie's chest.

Laurie fought for calmness, afraid of offending Ev

if she withdrew her hand, moved away, got up, left the room, never returned. She struggled to keep her head clear as her heart rammed blood through her veins. Her ears roared with each beat. *Swoosh, swoosh, swoosh.*

"Well, I'm kind of a rut person," she said by way of conversation. "I find something I like and it's hard for me to change."

"That explains why you've kept that same old ratty-looking cowboy hat since the day you first visited here. It's a wreck and outdated, you know."

"Right." Ev's breast pressed against Laurie's arm. For all her muscles, Ev had remarkably soft breasts. Laurie chided herself. What'd she expect the woman to have, two rocks protruding from her chest? Just because the rest of Ev was as solid as granite that didn't mean her breasts would be too. After all, Ev *was* a woman. "God!" Laurie started to rise, but Ev yanked her back down.

"Goddamn it, Laurie. Stay here."

"No!"

"Yes!" Ev gripped her again. "Yes. I need you to be here with me. I *need* you, Laurie. I need to be held, to hold, to stop feeling like I'm just out there alone, floating around with no anchor. You can give me a moment for that, can't you, for Christ's sake?"

Very reluctantly, Laurie agreed. "All right, Eveleen, I'll stay for a while, but then I must go."

Laurie felt warm tears collecting against her cheek as she turned toward Ev and pulled her close. Feeling silly, Laurie had to adjust her own large breast with her hand so that Ev didn't roll onto her. More movements and shifting and they fit together nicely. Laurie found herself most comfortable with one knee

110

bent and resting across Ev's. Ev seemed complacent with a leg wedged between Laurie's knees as she tucked her head beneath Laurie's chin and exhaled deeply. A shudder shook her, and Laurie placed a hand on her friend's hair, stroking her, whispering reassuring words and rubbing her back. Ev seemed to settle down.

During their college years, Laurie had never held Ev this way. It felt good to embrace a friend — this friend. She bet she could have held Ev like this back then, too. It would have been nice, rather like holding a needy child. But this was no child in her arms. This was an adult.

She dozed off, awaking from time to time. Ev hadn't moved. In a great burst of love for her, Laurie experienced a pleasant surge of warmth spreading throughout her chest, into her belly and radiating down her legs. It alarmed her, and then she remembered just who she was. She was the woman who was comforting her best friend.

With things set in proper perspective, her body tensions eased while her thoughts calmed themselves, allowing her to candidly acknowledge the conscious pleasure Ev's nearness generated within her. They were pleasing sensations, acceptable expressions of emotion. Unquestionably, she was enjoying friendship at its most powerful level. That's all, she told herself. Nothing more.

She rested for longer than she should have before returning to Grandma's room. Grandma lay awake, staring at the wall painting of a plains woman gathering wildflowers with one hand and holding a rifle and her horse's reins in the other.

"I checked on Ev, Grandma. She's asleep."

111

"Took you long enough, but that's good, too."

It was a half-hearted rebuff on Grandma's part. Laurie suppressed a smile, not wanting to evoke a real rebuke from her. Seated again, she refilled her mug. The coffee was cold now. It didn't matter so long as it was coffee.

"Did you talk with her at all?" Grandma asked. She picked at the blanket with little pecking motions.

"Not much. Just to say goodnight. She's pretty sad."

"She say why?"

"No, not specifically."

"She's all right. Glad you checked in on her."

Laurie nodded. "It's you I worry about, Grandma. It's the middle of the night and you know you should be sleeping." Laurie shifted to the bed, taking Grandma's hand.

The elderly lady lay unmoving for a moment. "I'm old. Don't worry about me. I don't need anybody worrying over me anymore."

Laurie caught her breath. "Grandma, don't say that. We all need to worry about one another. Always. Even you. Especially you."

"No, child, I don't need anybody fretting over me. I need to tell you about my friends."

Laurie debated voicing her next comment and then plunged in. "I know you thought of Helena as your friend, but what did you think of her homosexuality?"

"Her what?"

Damn! Did Grandma know nothing of today's world? "Her . . . liking girls."

"Oh. Can't say I ever much thought about it one way or the other. Love's love, ain't it?"

112

"I'd have to give it some consideration."

"You do that, girl. Meanwhile, would you like to hear about Honora Rosland Unsworth?"

"I would, Grandma. But tell me, did all these people ever actually meet one another?"

"Eventually, dear, eventually."

Laurie returned to her seat and settled down. She had gained her second wind and bit into a slightly dried-out sandwich as Grandma's frail voice immediately began to lure her into the next hypnotic tale.

Chapter Thirteen
Honora, 1876

Honora Rosland Unsworth, wife of uniformed
Major Jeffery Simson, danced in absolute happiness in
the Great Ballroom of the luxurious Hotel Washington located on Pennsylvania Avenue. The Unsworths
loved to dance, frequenting the balls held in
Washington, and heaven knew there were always
plenty going on. She was glad he could make 1876's
military ball. He had been on barracks duty during
the previous two balls.

Offering drinks and sweets on large silver trays, servants moved adeptly among the swirling dancers and idle gossiping guests. Scores of lanterns and crystal chandeliers cast strong light throughout the ballroom and its anterooms. A full dress military band played waltzes, contra dances and reels.

Honora wore her finest gown, a lovely pastel green taffeta which, she thought, greatly set off her remarkable hazel eyes. The skirt billowed like a blooming bluebell from layers of starched petticoats worn beneath. She had delicate facial bones, a patrician nose, and had rouged her cheeks a faint pink and scented her breath with dried mint chewed to a pulp by strong white teeth. Unburdened by this past summer's sun's hot rays, her skin was as smooth as fresh settled cream. She wore forest green cotton gloves reaching to her elbows.

"Happy, darling?" Jeffery asked as he expertly twirled his wife around the floor.

"More than I can say." Honora knew she glowed with joy. She looked over his broad shoulder, searching for Danette, her best-loved friend in all the world. Spotting her several yards away, Honora thought she looked striking, entirely convinced that Danette could wear an old feed sack and still be utterly beautiful.

Danette danced gracefully in the arms of her devilishly handsome and bearded husband, Major Robert Evans Dunlop. High, dark brows and long black lashes accented Danette's deep blue eyes. Her shining golden hair was held back by a single pink ribbon. Her gown was a pale pink cut exceeding low to amply display the cleavage of her shapely white bosom. A single dark mole adorned her right breast just above the bodice. Throughout the evening's entertainment, Honora had observed countless men's eyes beholding the mark's position — as had Honora's. Danette wore no gloves, displaying well-formed arms and delicately structured hands.

She appeared to float on air as Robert led her effortlessly through the waltz. Honora finally caught Danette's eye and smiled. Danette returned the smile and gave a slight wave.

The Dunlops lived several miles outside of Washington. Fortunately the Unsworths lived right in the city, providing the couples ample opportunity to visit several times a year. The Dunlops stayed overnight if the weather indicated it would be prudent to do so, and when visiting in turn, the Unsworths stayed with the Dunlops for the very same reason.

Tonight's climate had turned cold and snowy for so early in November. In a day or two, likely the sky would clear and the sun would melt away any lingering snow. Until then, however, the Dunlops would be staying the night, and Honora would savor every extra moment with Danette.

The ball continued until midnight. Enclosed carriages drawn by matched teams of horses waited before the Grand Hotel to carry away its sweaty, exhilarated visitors. The snow was falling much more heavily than when the dance had commenced. The vehicles' side lamps barely cut into the night's bleak darkness.

Aided by a coachman, Honora and Danette pulled their hooded wool cloaks tighter around their shoulders and stepped inside the waiting carriage. They sat together, their skirts filling half the interior, and immediately began chattering nonstop about everything and nothing. Their husbands, cloaked in army blue, tugged at the brims of their hats and said little.

"I hate the way Susanne flirts," Danette said. "Rolling her eyes at the men like a frightened cow."

Honora doubled over with mirth as the carriage pulled away.

"Really, Honora," Jeffery said. "You're acting perfectly silly."

The lamps cast just enough light within the carriage to allow its passengers to see one another, but only barely. Honora looked not at Jeffery, but at Danette. A second wave of convulsions gripped her, and she rolled toward Danette, resting her head on her friend's shoulder as she roared over Jeffery's straight-laced behavior. "Oh, come now, Jeffery," she said between bursts of giggles. "This is a night to have fun. So, have fun."

He shook his head and glanced at Robert.

"You too, Robert," Danette said, chuckling. "You look as stern as an old general."

"Don't poke fun at me, Danette," he pronounced. "Anymore, every time you two females get together you embarrass me."

Danette stilled. "Ahhh, that's why I didn't talk with Honora barely a bit this evening. You old war horses planned it that way."

Honora laughed until she thought her corset stays would snap in half. "That's funny, Jeffery." She continued giggling until she said, "I think I'm going to be sick."

"Good heavens, Honora, straighten up." He looked thoroughly disgusted with her. "You've been behaving like a child since —"

"I know," she said raising her hand to stop his flow of words. "Since I learned that Danette and Robert were staying the night."

"And maybe tomorrow night, too," Danette chimed in. "I think we should stay no matter what the weather, don't you, Robert? We could all take in a play or a concert."

Robert removed his snow-white gloves and carefully placed them on his knee. "That remains to be seen, darling. If the weather is good, we'll go home."

"No, not yet, Robert. Please." Danette reached across and took his hand. "Honora and I will straighten up, won't we, Honora?"

Honora burst out laughing again. "Yes, yes, of course. As soon as I grow up." She spewed spittle in a vain attempt to contain her laughter.

"Tomorrow, we leave!" Robert turned to Jeffery. "I apologize for my wife's part in all this silliness, Jeffery. She used to be so level-headed."

"Never were these two level-headed when they were together," Jeffery answered.

"Oh, posh," Danette answered sharply. "You're both too serious anymore. It was one of the very things you boys used to enjoy about our friendship. We laughed. And you laughed too."

Exasperated beyond measure, Honora tossed back her hood and crossed her arms in a huff, gazing without seeing through the carriage window. Then, unable to help herself, she began chuckling again.

"Be still!" Jeffery glared at her.

"All right, darling," she said complacently. "I'll behave as you wish." It would be easy to be genteel now. He had removed her last traces of giddiness.

The remaining journey was subdued as the men

quietly exchanged army anecdotes. Honora looked at nothing through the window, occasionally glancing toward Danette, who looked her way, too.

Once home, everyone's mood lifted. Jeffery started a fire in the parlor where they would meet after changing into more comfortable attire.

The Unsworth house was modest with the parlor and an efficient kitchen downstairs and three small bedrooms upstairs.

In their room, Jeffery sat on the edge of the bed struggling with his boots. Freed of them, he dropped them noisily to the floor, then removed his uniform, carefully hanging it in the closet. Beneath the decorative ensemble of numerous colorful medals, polished black leather and shining brass buttons, he wore long, drab gray underwear. "You were terrible in the carriage tonight, Honora. You humiliated me."

Never one to stay angry or sad for long, Honora eyed him up and down. Gone were the strong contours of his frame so nicely set off by his outfit. In its stead were baggy elbows and knees and the underwear's buttoned bottom, which hung as though he carried ten pounds of grain in the seat. He was still fussing with his uniform, his back to her. If he turned around she would have to fight a threatening smile. These days, the only funny thing about Jeffery was his underwear.

"Oh, Jeffery, you must learn to relax, especially tonight. I'm just so happy this evening. Don't penalize me for that. Our friends are here. It's time we all laughed together." He stared skeptically at her. "It is." She refused to be intimidated by him. "Come, Danette and Robert are probably already downstairs."

She quickly shed her evening gown, petticoats and

corset, tossing them over a chair, then pulled on a flannel nightdress. Contentedly, she scratched her breasts and hips.

Jeffery watched with disapproval. "Aren't you going to at least hang up your gown?"

"Time for that later. Let's go."

"You should do it now." He looked in the bureau mirror and gave his hair a quick brushing.

She bit her lip until she felt her teeth sink into her flesh. She shook out the gown before hanging it next to his uniform. "Satisfied?" she asked brightly.

"Thank you. You'll be glad you took care of it now instead of waiting until later."

No, she would not be glad later. He was stealing priceless time from her, from her time to be with Danette. He had become "army" to the degree that she could no longer bear him sometimes. "Let's go, Jeffery." She left him to follow behind.

The Dunlops were already waiting. Danette sat on the horsehair-upholstered couch in a loose, brown wool dress. Robert, in nightshirt and bathrobe, knelt before the fire, adding another log.

"Wine?" Jeffery offered, going immediately to a small cherry cabinet. He was dressed similarly to Robert. He drew out four glasses, setting them on the counter.

"Brandy," Robert said.

Honora assisted Jeffery, pouring wine for Danette and herself, brandy for the men.

Jeffery and Robert settled themselves on the couch placed before the fire. Their wives perched themselves on a large, braided rag rug, leaning comfortably against their husbands' shins. The men chatted amiably, again discussing war and politics

120

while the women listened and gazed into the warm flames.

Jeffery stroked Honora's hair as he said to Robert, "When we moved the settlers, they shot four soldiers before they were caught and hung."

Honora hadn't heard this story before. "You hung settlers?" she asked incredulously.

"I didn't," he said. "The army did. The settlers were paid well to move and given mules and wagons to do it with. They should have gone instead of murdering soldiers."

"Couldn't the railroad build around them?" Danette asked.

"They could," Jeffery explained. "But that's extra time, money and labor."

"But why take from those already established?" Danette asked.

"They shouldn't have had to move," Honora said. "Plain and simple, they were there first. Had they proved up the land?"

Her father had once looked into such a move. The Homestead Act of 1862 allowed a man to claim one hundred and sixty acres of the public domain. All he had to do was to live on his claim and farm it for five years. But her father learned that where he wished to homestead no trees grew to enable a man to build a home — which also meant no wood for fuel. About the only thing he found attractive after he had thoroughly studied the matter, he told his wife and daughter, was the cheap cost of land at a dollar twenty-five cents per acre. "A ridiculous undertaking for a man of my age," he said. Honora recalled her and Mother's intense relief when Father had at last laid his adventuresome thoughts aside.

"Most had," Jeffery said. "Those who hadn't had no choice but to move. Eminent domain," he added.

"Ridiculous," Honora said.

Danette nodded, indicating her displeasure as well.

At two, the men finally ran out of words. Not so the women, who had barely had an opportunity to say anything. Honora waited with concealed impatience for them to depart. Alone, she and Danette could have a good talk.

"I must go to bed," Jeffery said. "It's been a long day." He stood and stretched, the others rising with him.

"I'll be along, Jeffery," Honora said. She was *not* going to go with him now. "You and Robert have dominated the conversation all evening long. Now it's Danette's and my turn. That is, if you'd care to, Danette?"

Straight-faced, she nodded. "That would be fine with me."

They were left to their senseless chatter. As he made his way upstairs, Jeffery called down, "Come to bed soon, Honora."

"I will, dear." She would probably see the sun rise.

"You too, Danette. Don't be long." Robert's voice, too, floated down the stairwell.

"Of course," Danette called.

The women remained frozen until they heard both bedroom doors click.

Happiness gripped them as they clutched each other, dancing in tiny circles before the fire. Honora fought from squealing with delight.

They returned to the rug, their backs to the

couch. Honora drew her dress to her knees, allowing the delicious heat radiating from the flames to warm her skin. Wine warmed her stomach. Danette's closeness warmed her heart.

"He bores me silly, sometimes, Honora," Danette said as she gazed into the fire.

"Lately, it's been nothing but the same old stories every time they get together," Honora answered.

Danette agreed. "I hope Robert wants to stay another day. He gave me quite a tongue-lashing for my foolishness in the carriage."

"Jeffery had a word or two to say to me, too. Why are men like that, Danette? When does the joy go out of their hearts? When do they lose that boyish charm that captures women so readily?"

"Maybe it's something they're born with that manifests itself as they mature — like taking things from people or going off to war."

"They're way too controlling, if you ask me." Honora pulled her skirt down and drew her knees to her chest. She hugged them and leaned lightly against Danette's side. "Perhaps if I'd served in a war or had seen someone hanged or threw somebody off their land in the name of freedom or expansion, I might become cheerless, too."

"Don't forget greed." Danette carefully placed another log on the fire. Bright sparks flew up the chimney as the log disturbed those already burning. She returned to sit tightly against her friend.

Honora's heart clicked from canter to gallop. "It isn't right."

"What isn't?" Danette's eyes danced in the flickering light. Honora studied the silken lashes.

"All of it. War, land grabs, eminent domain. Yes, and greed. It'll crush this country one day, and if not the country then thousands of people's lives."

"I'm sure you're right."

Honora felt herself being drawn into Danette. She took a deep breath, then shyly asked, "May I put my arm around you, Danette?" Her face, already warmed by fire and wine, heated to near discomfort.

"It would please me greatly if you did." Danette smiled at her, dissolving Honora's heart into a puddle of sweet honey as she slipped her arm around Danette's waist.

What pleasant feelings a woman can give, Honora thought. Several minutes of silenced followed. "This is so nice," she said. She rested her head against Danette's shoulder as Danette took her hand.

"Your skin is so soft." Danette's voice took on the quality of velvet. Honora could have listened to the timbre of it for the rest of her life. Lucky, lucky Robert.

They remained unmoving for some time, Honora deeply content as Danette massaged her palm.

Without leaving the confines of Danette's arm, Honora turned her face toward Danette. Danette's gaze locked itself upon Honora's. How satiny she looks, Honora thought. And her lips, even more so. Shadows caressed Danette's high cheekbones, accenting her fine narrow chin.

Honora felt herself being lifted out of her body to stand beside the fire and observe the two women sitting so closely together. From her new position she watched as she placed her hand on the back of Danette's head. "Your hair is like silk," she said.

The pink ribbon still contained the thick tress.

Honora drew on one end. The satin strip fell away. Danette's hair cascaded down her back and over her shoulders. Honora wove her fingers through golden gossamer strands. Unmoving, Danette's gaze remained bound to Honora's.

Honora returned to her body. "How foolish I am," she said, slowing withdrawing her hand.

Danette bent to Honora's lips, kissing her fully and completely, and Honora returned the kiss as though it were the most natural act in the world, as natural as silver ripples expanding upon the surface of a placid lake.

Without surprise or question about what a remarkable thing they were doing, they openly gave themselves to each other, tongues touching, searching. They kissed a second time and began to pull and tug at each other. Danette lowered Honora to the rug as their breathing became tiny mews of pleasure and gentle gaspings. They explored soft shoulders and sides and backs.

"I love you so much, Honora. I have forever." Danette tenderly bit Honora's earlobe, then probed her ear with the tip of her tongue.

"I . . ." Honora was incapable of speaking. She slipped the upper half of her dress down to her waist and lay back on the floor. Danette rose and, like a pliable cloud of fog, resettled herself over Honora. "I need you, Danette." Honora kissed her deeply, the way Jeffery had never kissed her. She felt Danette return the kiss, as a gift, seeking her soul, caressing her spirit, caring how she felt. Honora pressed her palms against Danette's breasts feeling as though she might faint from rapture. "Oh, God, Danette," she whispered. She pulled up Danette's skirt and slipped her hand inside Danette's undermost garment. Thick, soft hair caressed her hand.

"For you, my beloved." Danette kissed her again. Her lips sought Honora's breasts and hardened nipples.

A cadence of pulses began in Honora's most private parts. "I think something wonderful is going to happen to me," she whispered. "I've never felt so desirous before."

"Neither have I, darling," Danette murmured against Honora's breast. She chewed on Honora's nipples, licking them, sucking them; shivers of ecstasy coursed through Honora.

Time passed, melted slowly away, became a useless thing. Honora needed only Danette's lips on hers, Danette's arms tightly holding her, her hands claiming her body. She longed to take Danette to her bed. The thought of it drove her to another bout of frenzied kissing.

Danette's hand cupped Honora. She slid a finger through downy hair and between moistened lips. Honora clutched her new lover, clawing at her back. She raised her hips, begging for more. "I want to feel you deep inside —"

"*What in God's name are you two doing? Have you both lost your minds?*" Jeffery stood towering over them, his face black with rage as stark disbelief and betrayal flooded his eyes.

Chapter Fourteen
Laurie, 1960

Laurie exhaled an anxious breath. "I need fresh coffee, Grandma." Apparently Grandma did too. She smiled approvingly when Laurie picked up the empty pot and walked unsteadily to the kitchen. God, Grandma's stories were so compelling — and sad. The wall clock over the sink read three A.M. "You could have lied," she said to its face.

She stood at the sink musing over the women long since dead. It was impossible to picture them as dust in their caskets. Like a Goddess of Creation, Grandma had given each one life and breath, meaning and substance.

Suddenly she felt as if the women were watching her as she refilled the pot, walking with her while she rummaged through cupboards until she found the coffee. One of them, Laurie had no idea who, moved aside, staying close by but not in Laurie's way as she dumped old grounds in the garbage and poured fresh into the strainer.

She dropped the lid onto the pot and put it on the stove. Turning on the gas flame, she felt a hand cover hers. She felt, too, the heat bouncing off the pot's bottom. The apparition said, "Turn down the flame. Waste of gas."

Laurie listened and obeyed, then rested at the butcher's block, waiting for the water to boil.

"Coffee's probably ready now," she said to them. She was alert in a comatose way, awake and disbelieving but willing to go along with whatever her tired mind created.

No one spoke as she grabbed a couple of fresh cups and a cookie jar filled with molasses cookies. She put these on a tray.

"The pot," she was told.

"I know." She put the pot on the tray, too.

"It's very late."

"Grandma must be exhausted," Laurie answered.

"She is. Very. You must hurry."

Laurie's heart quickened. "Why?" she asked the ghostly specters surrounding her.

"She's very, very tired," the voices echoed.

Laurie hastened down the hallway, then paused at Grandma's door. Somehow the old woman had managed to discard the extra pillows that had kept her propped upright all night. She lay flat and still, her hands folded as though she were already laid out for viewing.

"Grandma?" Barely able to stifle her rising alarm, Laurie put the tray on the dresser, knocking over several photos in her haste. She scurried to Grandma's side.

"We warned you, Laurie. Hurry now," the voices urged.

"To where, good women, where am I to go?"

"Hurry, hurry . . .."

Their ghostly voices faded. Laurie experienced an overwhelming sensation of their standing so near her, she could practically reach out and touch them if only she could see them.

"They're here, ain't they, Laurie? Henry, Honora, Helena, Louisa. All of them. They're here and you saw them, didn't you?" Grandma's voice was weakening. She didn't sound like the same woman that Laurie had left not twenty minutes ago.

And Henry — again.

"No, Grandma, I didn't see them. I felt them. They spoke to me. I didn't feel the presence of a man. Only that of women." What would be the harm in letting her believe, too, that they were here? No, she didn't mean to say "too." That would mean *she* believed the dead women to be here instead of thinking that her mind was just plain exhausted and willing to accept any weird happenings going on tonight. She tried to laugh off the notion but failed, giving up trying to make sense of it all; she believed herself to be almost as tired as Grandma. Carefully, she sat beside the frail woman.

Grandma rolled her head toward Laurie. "What did they say?" Laurie had to lean close to Grandma's lips to hear her words.

"Not a lot," she answered.

"What?" Grandma gasped. "What did they say?" she asked in a voice weaker still.

Should Laurie tell her? Should she mention that she was advised to hurry to Grandma's side?

"Did they tell you anything?"

"No," Laurie lied. "One of them told me to turn the heat lower under the coffee pot."

"There was more. Tell me."

"I don't recall, Grandma."

"Get my Ev and her father. Hurry."

"Grandma, if you'll just sleep you'll —" A chill unlike any Laurie had ever before experienced fell upon her. She began to tremble uncontrollably.

"Laurie." Grandma's voice seemed stronger. Laurie wrapped her arms around herself and breathed deeply, closing her eyes while her mountain of fear rapidly grew. "One of them is here by my side, Laurie."

"Who, Grandma?"

"Why, look, child. Everybody is here."

Laurie guardedly opened her eyes. From the other side of the bed she felt frigid air blowing her way. "I don't see anyone, Grandma."

"Hello, Henry," Grandma said. "My, you're looking handsome this evening."

"Who's Henry, Grandma?"

Laurie watched Grandma listening as though someone were actually there and speaking to her.

"I miss you all very much," Grandma said. She

listened again, smiling, her lips folding in upon themselves and caving in her cheeks.

"What's going on, Grandma?" Laurie's voice was trembling badly.

"You'd better get Ev and Dad, Laurie. It's time." Grandma looked happy. Incredibly happy.

"Grandma . . ."

"Go, child. Right now. I'll wait."

Laurie paused, unable to believe that Grandma was actually failing. Her brain refused to accept such a possibility.

Grandma's arm shot out and slapped her on the thigh. It hurt as though she had been stung. She bit her lip to keep from crying out.

"I'm sorry, Laurie. That came from Henry. Says you're gonna get plugged if you don't hustle."

Laurie had no doubt that something terrifying would happen to her, more terrifying than was occurring right now, if she didn't move. She ran to Ev's room and threw on the light. Ripping aside the covers, she said, "It's Grandma, Ev. She's sent for you and Luke."

"What's happening?" Ev was already on her feet and running toward her father's room.

"I don't know. Grandma's failing for sure. She's hearing voices or something." Laurie raced behind her.

"Dad!" Ev had only to call him once. Dressed only in his shorts, he came flying from his room.

"Hi, Laurie," he said as he hustled by her. "When did you get here?" He didn't wait for an answer as the three of them entered Grandma's room. She was still intently observing the empty space beside her.

"They've come, Luke," she said.

"Oh, Grandma." His voice cracked. The pain he expressed in his two simple words did not fit this tall, rangy, gray-headed man. His ruddy complexion melted away, leaving his chiseled lips white and pinched at the corners. Laurie watched this normally rugged cowboy fight for control.

He sat on the bed beside his great-grandmother and took her hands in his large weathered ones. "Please."

Grandma answered in a stronger voice, "I'm a hundred and two, child. I can't live forever."

"You can," he said. "You're strong." He sounded like a frightened child. Tears fell from his eyes.

"Don't be silly, Luke. You've always been silly. Like a little boy."

Tenderly he kissed her cheek. "I love you so, Grandma. I love you so."

"I love you too, child. Now go and have a good life. Get married again. You need a wife."

"I just need you, Grandma."

"You'll marry again, son. And you'll be happy again."

He didn't argue, nor did he agree.

Laurie looked at Ev, who nodded that it would, indeed, happen.

Laurie thought she might vomit from fear and repeatedly swallowed back the coffee and sandwiches she had been consuming since early that evening. How could Grandma just say things and have people believe her? Ev did the same thing. Again, Laurie felt bitter cold descending upon her. She began to shake so hard she had to sit.

"Put a blanket around her, Ev," her father said.

Ev covered her friend with a comforter found in Grandma's closet.

"I need to speak to Ev for a minute, son. Laurie, you stay, too. Woman stuff, Luke." Grandma smiled weakly at him.

He nodded and started for the door.

"Please, Luke, stay." Laurie would be less afraid if he did. Life would seem more real, like what she knew life to be. Not this apparition kind of event permeating the room. She continued to shake and clasped her hands in her lap in an effort to gather herself into one small, controllable area.

"I'll be nearby," he promised, patting her shoulder. He stopped just beyond the threshold.

"Laurie."

Grandma's voice had changed, sounded younger, stronger. Its unexpected change caused Laurie to leap. She needed to get *out* of here. She threw off the comforter, intending to go.

"I love you, Laurie," Grandma whispered. The old woman's breath seemed to reach out to her, freeze her where she sat. "I didn't get to finish my stories. I thought I would but I didn't, so you got to listen to Ev now, just like you been listening to me, you understand? You listen good, now. I mean it."

"I will, Grandma," Laurie whispered, quivering. "And I love you, too."

Ev moved to Grandma's opposite side. "You'll have to finish the stories, darlin'."

Ev took her withered hand. "I will, Grandma. I won't leave out a word."

"It's important you get it right." Laurie's fear lessened as Grandma's voice returned to the languishing but crackling tenor she had listened to for the past several hours. "Don't be shy. Tell everything. You need to. Tell about Henry."

"I won't forget a thing, Grandma. I promise."

"I love you, Eveleen." Ev began to cry while arduously fighting not to. "We'll talk, darlin'."

"Of course, Grandma. Every day."

"Get Dad now."

Laurie and Ev moved to the end of the bed while Grandma spoked with her great-grandson until the light faded from her eyes and her chest no longer rose and fell.

"It's so quiet here anymore," Ev said. Two weeks had passed since Grandma's death. "I can hardly stand it." She and Laurie sat resting on the plains three miles away from the house. Their horses grazed nearby. Laurie listened to them grinding grass between their teeth, making juicy sounds.

"Very," Laurie agreed. "Very quiet, indeed."

Laurie recalled how busy it had been around here for several days following Grandma's death. The grand and ancient woman was laid to rest beside the last of her three husbands, all of whom were buried side-by-side in the family plot. Her funeral had been attended by Luke and Ev, most of the ranch-hands, Miriam and Pauline and Laurie. A few town officials were there as were some of the ladies from the Baptist church, a church which Grandma never once attended. A preacher she had never met delivered the eulogy.

Dozens of covered dishes were delivered by ladies of surrounding ranches. Through the days, Laurie listened to the cooks grumble at the food, wondering what they should do with it all, but they complained only to cover the loss of someone they had both greatly loved. Men from other spreads volunteered their time to help run the ranch while Luke and his family got through these difficult days. Dozens of sympathy cards and letters arrived from all over the United States. Grandma had been so old, and people seemed overly impressed with the fact.

A gentle breeze across the prairie blew strands of Laurie and Ev's hair about their faces. Ev looked like a sun-bronzed statue, rigid and unmoving except when she spoke. Several minutes passed before she said, "I should get on with finishing Grandma's stories for you, Laurie. It's been a while."

Laurie grunted. Three dead women, and now Grandma too. And she couldn't forget Henry. No doubt she would hear about him one day. Perhaps he had been one of Grandma's lovers. Grandma had been so tough, outliving her husbands, her children and several boyfriends. Laurie had heard about some of the boyfriends but not all.

But how real the women had become. Remarkably, Laurie missed them. She thought about their meager hopes, their great defeats, their shattered lives. When had they come together to have their picture drawn? How did they meet? Surely not in an asylum for the insane. Not all of them. None were insane. Perhaps a little warped in their thinking — the lesbians at least — but not the religious one. How had it ended for them? There was more to hear, to learn. Someday, maybe. Not today. Not now. Perhaps next year.

But why should Laurie bother listening any longer? She had done it now and in the past mainly for Grandma's sake. And damn it, why must Ev be so much like the old woman, and in some ways, seem to become her? Why couldn't she and Ev just have good times again like they'd always had each and every year?

"I could start now," Ev suggested brushing dust from her pants and green checkered shirt. Her well-worn hat lay at her side.

"Is it so important that I know?"

"Yes." Ev looked off into space. She seemed to close in upon herself. "I promised Grandma."

"You promised to tell me. I didn't promise to listen. Why don't you put it on a tape recording and send it to me and then I could listen when —"

"You won't. You won't ever listen unless I personally tell you."

"Of course I would, Ev. If I say I will, I will."

"No, you won't. You'll get back to Cleveland and your demanding job, and of course, Joe. Your life will be completely filled and you won't have time. Oh, your intentions will be good, but you'll keep putting it off and putting it off until having to listen to the tape becomes a chore, a thing you feel you *have* to do. Then it'll be something you hate to have to do, and you won't." She looked at Laurie with something in her eyes that Laurie couldn't read. "And you'll hate yourself for having put it off for so long. You'll hate that you hadn't done it sooner and gotten it over with." She stared out across the prairie. "A tape won't do."

Shame scorched Laurie's face. Of course. Ev could see straight through her. Had for years. "I hate that you can read my mind, Ev. That's what I hate. Who did you inherit that . . . that thing from? Your dad, through your great-great-grandmother? Grandma had it, didn't she? I know she did."

Ev turned slowly and looked into Laurie's eyes, reaching down into her, touching her somewhere deep within, someplace unfamiliar to Laurie. "It's just that I know you so well. Nothing else."

Laurie frowned, not believing her. She rolled up the sleeves of her tan cotton shirt, then leaned back on one elbow, stretching her long, lean Levi-covered legs. Pulling up a blade of grass, she stuck it in her mouth. The blade was sharp, cutting her lip as she drew it between her lips. "Ouch!"

"Don't eat that stuff," Ev told her, smiling. "It's for horses and cattle."

Laurie smiled back. "Dumb cowgirl, I am."

"City lights, country candles. Some mixture you got in you, gal."

"I love both."

"You ought to live out here, Laurie."

Laurie scanned the sun-drenched plains before her. How beautiful was this land. How wonderful it felt beneath her boots as she took her morning walks. She wondered what it would be like to live here for years on end as Ev had done. Would she become bored? Would her eyes grow weary from the unbroken horizon? Its lack of trees? Only reluctantly did the Kansas earth relinquish its wealth, insisting that man fight for every inch of soil, every blade of grass, every drop of water.

"Sometimes I think you're right. But Joe would never move here. Not enough houses to paint."

"He's a city boy anyway."

"Born and bred. He absolutely loves Cleveland."

"I could never live in the city. I hated college.

Loved the courses, but the city felt like it was beating down on me all the time. Like a bad storm that never quits."

"I never knew that."

Ev stretched out alongside Laurie and brushed wayward chocolate strands of hair from her eyes. "I never mentioned it. Sounded too much like complaining."

Miffed, Laurie answered, "Well, you could have complained. I would have listened."

"If it suited you."

Laurie sat up. "Ev McNelly, I would too have listened. I've always listened to you, and you know it."

"But — not now."

Laurie stared into Ev's eyes.

"I'm right, then."

"All right, Ev. I'll listen. But I'm frightened of what I'll hear. I'm scared to death thinking I might be surrounded by ghosts at night. I'm a grown woman, but honest to God, Ev, I'm scared shitless." She scowled, genuinely concerned.

Ev smiled at her. "No one's here at night anymore, Laurie. Or in the day either. Not dead people, anyway." She reached out and took her friend's hand. "They've left. They were here to get Grandma."

"Good God, Ev. This is all in your imagination." Angrily, Laurie withdrew her hand. She absolutely deplored patronization.

Ev ignored the rebuke. "I believe it, Laurie. The house is empty except for you, me, Dad and the cooks. That's it. Nobody else."

"That's not what the cooks are saying."

"They're trying to scare you. I'm the one to believe."

"Yes, I suppose you are. You've never lied to me, yet." A curious thought struck her. "Are you in any way related to any of the women that Grandma talked about?"

"No."

"Is that the truth?"

"Sure."

Laurie was going to get nothing more from Ev. People born with veils over their faces were secretive and strange. Very strange. "Well, I'll listen to you, Ev. But I will *not* listen to one word past ten o'clock at night."

Ev grinned. "Agreed. Might's well start now."

She lay back on the grass and propped her hands behind her head while Laurie rolled onto her stomach, preparing herself for a long session. She selected another piece of grass and began chewing on it, taking care this time not to cut herself.

Chapter Fifteen
Sadie, 1870

Eighteen-year-old Sadie Riley tripped as her boot snagged in the hem of her linsey-woolsey. She would break her neck if she fell now. It was just plain foolishness to try to drag a four-hundred-pound, screaming, fighting-mad pig fifty yards from the barnyard to the butchering tree in an all-fired damn dress.

There was only Sadie and Pa to do the butchering each November because Claudia, her older sister, and

Rebecca, her younger, just sat and waited in the cabin until the pig was ready to be brought inside for cutting up. Every year it was the same old thing with those two no-account sisters turning squeamish and sick-like and 'bout ready to puke at the sight of blood. But they were ready enough to eat pork when it was set before them.

An energetic girl with bright brown eyes, Sadie was whip-thin and six feet tall. Her hair was plain brown and braided to keep it away from her face. Her mouth was strong, her cheeks hollow. She needed to put on an additional thirty pounds before she would take on any womanly qualities, but the way Pa worked her, it wasn't likely to happen until she was too blamed old to do anything but sit in a chair and knit.

She and Pa struggled with the squealing pig until Pa was able to stun it with a blow across its head using a heavy chunk of log. Quickly, Sadie bound strong hemp rope to each of the sow's rear legs, then tossed the ropes over a high strong branch. Grunting and straining against its weight, they hoisted the animal several feet into the air and tied the rope to the tree.

Sadie left Pa to finish off the sow. Later she would help him lower it into a large cauldron of boiling water, then scrape the bristles from its hide. As tasty as the meat would be this winter, she looked forward to the day when she would never have to be a part of killing anything in her life again, but it looked like that might be forever.

That evening, she lay awake in the loft of the cramped, drafty two-room cabin waiting for Claudia and Rebecca to fall asleep. The three of them wore long flannel nightgowns, wool nightcaps and socks. Eventually they breathed heavy and steady.

She rose and picked up her boots, slipping them on when she got outdoors. Without wool blankets and her sisters' warm bodies lying next to her, the night felt bitter cold. Puffs of breath steamed out before her and tears formed at the corners of her eyes.

The sky was clear; stars glowed like early-summer fireflies. She admired their brilliance, thinking how she would like to grab a few and put them in a jar to light up the dark cabin for Ma, the place being as gloomy as the inside of Miller's Cave over near Acretown.

A chill began to settle in her bones. To stay a little warmer, she wrapped her arms around her thin chest. At the butchering tree she pulled a rag from the pocket of her nightgown and rubbed it against the inside of a bucket used earlier for catching the pig's blood. The moon was bright enough so that she could easily see that the cloth was smeared good enough. She left it lying beside the hole in the outhouse.

Morning came early in the Riley cabin. Sadie woke up to Ma's timid voice calling from the foot of the ladder. "You girls git up out of there and git down here. We got to git this meat ground up. You come on, now. Claudia, Sadie, Rebecca. Come on." She sounded as though she hoped no one would holler at her for waking them. None of the girls ever did, knowing that their pa did enough yelling for all of them, and at just about anything that moved and a whole lot of things that didn't.

The girls groaned and mumbled and rolled out of their warm bed. It was like facing death, Sadie thought as she tossed her boots and clothes below before climbing down. Every morning, she and her sisters dressed before the fire Ma already had roaring in the big fireplace. They huddled together, yanking on their clothing as quickly as they could.

As one, the four women looked toward the door as Pa came in stomping his feet and shouting like a crazy man, "Who in hell left this filthy rag out'n the backhouse?" He displayed it for all to see.

Faster than quicksilver, Claudia answered, "Not me, Pa."

"Me, neither," Rebecca replied just as quickly.

Ma would never have done such a careless thing, and that left only Sadie to blame. All eyes fell upon her as she prepared herself for Pa's tongue-lashing.

"It's a filthy thing you done, Sadie Riley. You shame your ma and your sisters. You make yourself out to be a dirty, shameful girl no better 'n a whore." The girls scattered as he stalked over to the fireplace and flung the rag into the flames. It smoldered slowly, angering Pa further. "Goddamn thing," he snarled, trying to kick it farther into the fire.

Rebecca and Claudia scurried around making an effort to look busy and helpful. Ma silently began turning pig gut inside out, readying it for sausage casing. Sadie stood near the wood slab table, looking properly contrite, hanging her head and shuffling her feet. "Yes, Pa," she told him, sounding as shameful as she could.

It was over for another year.

Pa slammed out the house as Claudia began scolding Sadie, picking up where Pa had left off and like Ma should have been doing. Looking appropriately indignant, Claudia resembled a small school-marm with a switch in her hand. What she really held was nothing but a plain old wooden stirring spoon. She pointed it at her inconsiderate, empty-headed sister like she was going to clobber her with it. "Sadie Riley, you got pudding for brains, I swear. You don't never learn a blamed thing."

Nineteen and older than Sadie by a mere nine months, she was Sadie's hated sister. Sadie wasn't so hostile toward her that she couldn't still see that Claudia was as pretty as a clear rising dawn with her long yellow hair and shining blue eyes and delicate-boned body. Even dressed in plain old calico, Claudia turned heads. Sadie thought she put on airs, acting like the Queen 'a England, when she didn't even know what the Queen 'a England looked like. The thing Sadie most disliked about Claudia was her behaving as though she was years wiser than she actually was — all because she had been "a-bleeding" since she was eleven and Sadie herself only since she was fourteen.

But that wasn't true either. Sadie hadn't started bleeding at all. Sick and tired of hearing how they were already women and she was still nothing but an itty-bitty child, even though at fourteen she was taller than any of them except Pa, she took it in her head to bloody a rag using pig's blood. She'd leave it in the backhouse for somebody to find, then they would think she was a woman too, and let up on her. So far her scheme had worked, but she hated Pa's yearly scoldings, since he already laid plenty on her.

"Blamed fool girl," Rebecca said, taking Claudia's side while Ma just kept on turning pig gut inside out and looking nowhere but down at the slimy innards in her hands.

Rebecca was a year younger than Sadie, but she too behaved as if she was a whole lot older. Rebecca was nowhere near as pretty as Claudia. Her hair was thin and stringy like Ma's, and she carried bags under her light brown eyes that Sadie thought ought not to be there for someone so young. Her face was long and drawn, and her eyes lacked life, also just like her ma's. Rebecca had spent most of her seventeen years being sick. But she had a strong mind. She was smart, that one.

Sadie pulled on her leather boots, unable to stand the cold, hard-packed floor that was nothing but dirt.

"Gotta chink logs today, too, girls," Ma said, speaking quietly. "Along with everything else." She sounded as tired as Methuselah and had as far back as Sadie could remember.

"I'll do it, Ma," she volunteered, "soon's I milk the cow."

Ma barely nodded. She took a minute to stir something in the big cook pot already hanging over the fire.

Sadie looked into the cauldron and took a deep whiff of its bubbling contents. "What you cooking, Ma? Smells real good."

"Beans 'n pork." Ma spoke with little enthusiasm. Sadie suspected that Pa had been after her again last night.

"Well, it'll be real good, Ma," Sadie told her. She patted Ma's bony back, feeling her spine sticking out like points on a fancy picket fence. "Nobody cooks up beans the way you do."

Sadie was always quick to encourage her ma and tell her nice things. She was prompt and willing to do jobs her sisters wouldn't do and Pa didn't always have time for, such as stuffing cracks between logs and splitting and hauling firewood, plowing and planting. Claudia and Rebecca weren't much inclined toward outdoor work, a severe disappointment to Pa. But Sadie had to give her sisters their due. They weren't lazy either and made all the family's clothes and washed them, too, and cooked good meals. They made better sausage than Sadie, a nasty job she loathed mightily.

Pa came back in long enough to have cornbread, fresh sausage and coffee before taking off for the smokehouse down in the woods near where last winter they'd chopped down and split hickory trees and left them to dry out. He'd be patching up the place after a year's weathering and winds. Later, he'd come back smelling like smoke from stoking up a good hickory fire for curing the meat, and then late in the evening, he'd need to check the smokehouse, leaving the milking to Sadie. For the time being she would happily chink logs while her sisters and Ma worked the pig.

About three o'clock, Martha Swanson and her ma pulled up in their buckboard to help with the sausage grinding and stuffing and cutting up the pork. Next week the Rileys would go over to their cabin about three miles down the road and help out doing the same thing.

Sadie was glad to bursting that Martha had come along. She wasn't sure until now if she would. Martha made Sadie feel like a real person. She never minded that Sadie was tall and skinny as a sick cat, and she loved Sadie's long braids and eyes browner than fresh-turned earth. She had laughed at Sadie all this past summer long when Sadie shot up so fast she hurt all over all the time. Before the summer was over, Sadie had to duck a smidgen to get through the cabin door.

Pa had begun looking at her as though she were peculiar or worse, making her feel just wretched. She couldn't think of anything worse than being six feet tall and a girl. But he was glad enough about her unusualness when it came to chopping logs and splitting rails, because she wasn't just tall, she was strong as a two-year-old filly.

At milking time that afternoon, Martha followed Sadie to the barn just like Sadie knew she would. She knew from the way Martha was eyeballing her that her heart was about to beat very, very hard.

No sooner had Sadie pulled the door shut behind them and they'd hung their lanterns on nails than Martha jumped her from behind, squealing and laughing and carrying on. Martha had a straightforward way of making old Sadie feel as wondrous as watching a new calf being born right before her eyes.

Martha Swanson was the only one in Sadie's life that kept her heart beating for meaning. And her heart did begin to batter against her ribs as she turned toward Martha's laughing blue eyes.

Yep, she was right. Martha was about to do it to her again.

Chapter Sixteen

"Hey, you she-cat," Sadie yelled at Martha. The horse and cow started snorting and shuffling their hooves at the commotion. Sadie swung Martha around and pulled her into her arms. She studied her for a moment, taking in her copper-colored hair, her intense blue eyes and lightly freckled cheeks. "My, you are comely," she said, tucking Martha's head beneath her chin, cherishing her thin frame packed tight against her.

Sadie kissed Martha hard and meaningfully, believing her heart might stop. Martha returned the kiss before breaking away and bolting up the ladder to the hay loft packed with fresh hay from three good cuttings this past summer. Sadie followed close on her heels, glancing up Martha's wool blue dress all the way.

They scrambled across the hay on their hands and knees to a spot they had scooped out some months before. Laughing, Martha collapsed on her back. Sadie pounced on top of her and wrapped her arms around her. Again they kissed, roughly and passionately. They liked it like that, kissing and grabbing and wrestling around like two fighting gamecocks. But it stopped being funny whenever they both started rocking their hips against each other with increasing fervor. Martha would wrap her legs around Sadie and their breathing would become short, fast gasps until one of them yelled and sometimes both of them yelled.

Sadie could feel excitement crawling up her legs and through her belly. Martha must have been feeling the same, her head thrown back and her eyes closed tight. She looked as though Sadie might be hurting her, but it wasn't true at all, because Martha was smiling, too.

They had pulled their skirts to their waists, their hands beneath each other's cumbersome underclothing. Sadie was sure that Martha's bosoms were softer than goose down feathers. It took her breath away every time she touched them or thought about them during the times they didn't see each other, which were way too many for Sadie's way of thinking.

Martha would be getting married come spring, and they both knew that after three years of playing married folk, their childhood game was about to end.

Sadie ached at the thought of it, but Martha wasn't willing to play games all her life, which left Sadie with no hope for their future. But for now, old Sadie'd do for Martha, and Sadie couldn't resist her.

They were pushing hard against each other. The cow's mournful lowing to be milked and the wind's whistle mingled with the familiar sound of Martha about to go over the edge and taking Sadie right along with her. A horse could have been dropped on her and Sadie wouldn't have felt it.

And then a horse did drop on her. Sadie soared a foot, the excitement draining from her as fast as milk from a bucket. Terrible pain replaced it.

"What the —"

Her words were cut off by another vicious whack. Pa stood over the two lovers raining blows down on Sadie's back with a stick thicker than a hoe handle. Struggling to her knees, she fended off Pa's blows as best she could, yelling, "Git, Martha, go on!" She hovered over Martha until the terrified young woman could slide from beneath Sadie and escape down the ladder.

"I'll kill you, you daughter of Sodom!"

"Quit, Pa," she yelled. "Quit!" She was on her feet, circling him while she stumbled around in the hay, trying to get to the ladder. Her back and arms ached where he had clouted her.

Sadie prayed Martha would be smart enough to get her ma and take off for home. There was no telling what Pa would do once he got in the house.

As soon as Sadie hit the floor of the barn, Pa was right there, too. Having just turned somewhere near sixty, he was still faster than a cat.

The stock's eyes rolled in their sockets, spooked

by the noise and thumping around. Sadie wanted to put her hand on the animals' hides to steady them, but Pa was already after her again, with threats and blows coming at her from all sides.

"I'll whup your evil ass," he hissed. "You ain't normal. You ain't no good. You're too danged tall to marry off and too dumb to know right from wrong." His eyes were little more than slits in his face, his shaggy beard loose and tangled, flapping against his chest. He gave a vicious tug at the hat covering his balding head, pulling it down so far his ears bent sideways at the top.

Sadie was more than just scared. She was becoming angry too, and trying not to because he was her pa. He swung another blow, just missing her head. She ducked and tripped backward, falling over a pitchfork left lying out. She went down as he delivered another couple of glancing belts across her head before she could stand again. At this rate, she would be dead before she could stop him.

Desperate and wild with rage from being beaten without mercy, she leaped to her feet to tackle him. He reared back, raising the stick over his head, his eyes glazed and wild. He looked determined to kill her, either forgetting or not caring that she was his daughter and his best hand, including those he hired from time to time.

As the stick arced down, she grabbed the weapon-bearing arm in mid-swing before latching onto his free arm. There they were, the two of them, Sadie with tears streaking down her face and Pa cursing and spitting at her, as they grappled with and against each other.

Years of physically demanding labor had hardened

and strengthened Sadie, and although she wasn't winning the battle, she wasn't caving in either. Sweat poured from both their faces and their neck muscles knotted up to look like year-old saplings.

She hadn't ever paid attention before, but she discovered she was looking down on him. Why, she was better than a half-foot taller than he, his eyes looking like big black holes in his face except for the pinpoint of lantern light dancing out of each one, resembling sparks from hell. It scared her so badly she thought about releasing her hold.

She had never heard of a daughter and pa fighting before; only of daughters and sons getting caned good by their fathers. She had been caned plenty lately, it seemed. Every time she was late getting the milking done or hadn't stacked enough firewood for Ma, or just because Pa felt like it. He'd always been mean as sin, but he'd never licked her like this before and never since she'd grown door-ducking tall.

"You ain't a-gonna beat me no more, Pa," she said through clenched teeth in as normal a voice as she could manage. She was trying to be respectful, trying to make things natural again. "I ain't taking no more."

"I'll kill you for what you done."

"I ain't done nothing."

"You been a-fucking a girl." His breath came out smelling strongly of corn liquor. He'd been out working the still today, too.

"I ain't been doing no such thing," she lied. "Martha and me was just playing."

"You ain't young'uns. You was a-fucking her."

They remained face to face, or as face to face as

possible, Sadie looking down and he looking up, and his eyes definitely telling her he could kill her for it.

The thought must have been in his mind because he said in an awful low voice, "I'm gonna kill you, girl. You ain't normal."

He scared her then, and she could feel him gaining strength enough to do it. She clung to his wrists, throwing her full weight against him, catching him by surprise. He sprawled backward, stumbling over his own feet, going down hard.

In a wink, she yanked up her dress, freeing a knee, and knelt heavily against his throat. His eyes started bulging out as he swung the stick again, but the wind had been knocked out of him, and he didn't have much strength left to hit her hard as the weapon connected with the back of her head.

"Damn you, you mean old man," she screamed. Spit flew from her mouth, hitting his face. "You're never gonna smack me again." She yanked the stick from his hand and threw it as far as she could. His eyes looked ready to explode out of their sockets. If she knelt on him much longer, he'd be dead. She gasped for air, so tired and sore that she was sure she was going to keel over sideways. She rolled him onto his back and knelt on his neck as she snatched a piece of rope from a nail. She tied his hands behind his back and said hoarsely, "I just want you to leave me be. But I know it ain't in your nature to be kind to anything, living or dead, so I'm gonna tie you up, and maybe you'll just lay right here till you freeze to death. But I'll be gone by then." Her hands trembled so much, she wasn't sure she'd tied the rope well enough and took the time to retie it.

"You'll have to hire you another hand, if'n you live. Claudia and Rebecca ain't likely to help you like old Sadie here always done." She bound his feet as well. He wasn't going anywhere till somebody let him loose. "And you can't be using Ma like you do, neither. You been using her till she's 'bout all gone. She's gonna die if'n you don't let up on her." She panted like a wounded animal as she spoke, hating him and hating herself even worse for fighting with him.

Throughout the commotion, the horse and cow had pranced restlessly on the edge of panic. Sadie was relieved to see them settling down as she tied Pa to a beam so he couldn't hop after her. That done, she lit out of the barn as fast as she could.

Bruises covered her head, back and arms. She wouldn't be able to move right for a month. Somehow, Pa missed hitting her in the face. She was sure grateful for that. She'd hate to have Martha see how bad a whipping she'd taken.

In the cabin, Martha sat at the table, still as death and looking scared out of her head. Sadie gave her a wink to make her feel better, but her face didn't change a whit.

"Ma," Sadie said, going over and kneeling beside her. She and Mrs. Swanson sat on stools, resting before the fire, each of them staring into the flames while a dress Ma was repairing lay ignored in her lap. Pa's coon hound slept in a ball at their feet. Claudia and Rebecca were off in one corner knitting and talking about nothing like they were always doing, meaning that Martha had kept quiet.

The light from the fire etched deep lines in Ma's

face. "Ma," Sadie began again. "I gotta tell you something, and it ain't going to be nice."

Ma's face froze up as though she knew what was coming. She clasped her hands together and turned her frightened, fawn-like eyes upon Sadie. "Is Pa all right?"

Her first concern had always been Pa. Mean as he was, he kept food on the table. Sadie didn't know if Ma had strength enough to do it herself if she had to, and from looking at her, Sadie was sure she didn't.

"Pa's just fine," Sadie said. "But he's been caning me again and I can't take no more. I'm fixing to leave. Right now." She heard Martha's sharp intake of breath.

"I *got* to," Sadie said rising painfully and looking at Martha. "Pa's likely to kill me."

Claudia and Rebecca were up now, too, with their mouths opened wide enough to swallow a calf but keeping still for once.

"What you done, child?" Ma asked. She looked more and more scared, her body tensing up like a set bear trap.

"I ain't done nothing, Ma, nothing at all. Me and Martha here was up in the loft laughing and talking and carrying on like two little chillun, and Pa came up and started caning me for not doing my work. He . . . he accused me and Martha of some awful acts, Ma, and they just ain't true."

"What acts?" The dress slipped from Ma's lap without her noticing.

"I ain't never heard of them before," Sadie said. "I don't know what he's talking about, but he sure is mad. I should have just been milking the cow and not playing." She took Ma's knotty hand, with its thick knuckles and thicker palms, in her own and looked into her hopeless gray eyes. "He's truly mad, Ma. But I ain't going to stand for his caning me no more. I'm leaving right now."

"You ain't a-goin' anywhere, girl." Ma sounded good and mad herself, bringing Sadie up short. Ma hardly ever got mad at anything. "You're a-goin' to march right back into that barn and tell your pa you're sorry. Him that's fed you all your life and put clothes on your back."

Her words came as no surprise. She had always backed him against her girls, but scared as Sadie was to disobey, she couldn't do what Ma asked.

"I'm leaving, Ma. I got to and that's that."

Ma argued and started crying, but Sadie'd said all she was going to.

Hanging on a nail in one corner of the cabin next to Ma and Pa's rope and cornshuck bed where they'd slept for the past twenty-five years, Pa kept the extra pair of brown wool pants he wore for Sunday meeting and funerals. Sadie grabbed them and his only other wool shirt, buttoning it to her neck. She hurried to the loft and changed, then stuffed her pockets with a knife and pocketwatch a peddler passing through had swapped for a gallon of corn liquor she'd swiped from Pa's still. She took a blanket instead of her coat, fearing hers would be too easy to spot. Final items were a comb and her wool nightcap for a hat.

Downstairs, Martha remained frozen at the table. Mrs. Swanson hadn't spoken a word since Sadie had come in. It was unlikely she would get mixed up in her neighbor's business, even though her daughter was involved. She, like everyone else in the county, knew how outrageous Pa's anger and accusations could be.

Sadie watched her ma pacing around empty-headed-like in the cabin's small interior, whimpering and wringing her hands. Her sisters held each other's hands, their mouths still hanging open like they had busted hinges on their jaws. Neither one of those sissies would ever take up her side.

There was nothing else for her to do here. She couldn't change a thing — Pa's beating her, Ma's sorry lot in life, her sisters' timid ways. And Martha — that dream ended with Pa's first blow across Sadie's back. She wanted to cry, to throw herself in Ma's arms and have Ma tell her everything was going to be all right. It would be, but only if she got herself out of there.

"I'm going now, Ma." She wanted to at least hug her ma before leaving, but Ma wouldn't stop roaming and turned her back on her.

She wanted to hug her sisters, too, but they moved to Ma's side. Sadie knew what they were thinking. She was crazy and would be back in an hour.

The hound looked up at her with mournful eyes. Sadie walked over to him and patted his head. She would have liked to take him along for company, but that would be an added problem, and she needed to travel as fast and as far away as she could get, even if it meant not stopping before next week Sunday.

Martha picked up her coat and rushed after Sadie, who was already out the door and heading down the road. She finally caught up with her. "You ought not to run away, Sadie." Tears glistened in her eyes, the moon making them look like two big pools of silver. "How'll you get by? A girl can't go off by herself."

"I ain't a girl no more, Martha. I'm a man. A young man. I can move around better that way, I think."

"A man?"

"I think I can do it. Anyway, I can't stay here no more. You just back up my story and you'll be all right. Just make like Pa's crazy. It's your word and mine against his. Everybody knows how he's always beating me, and for no good reason. They'll believe you. You'll be all right," she said again.

"I know, but I'll miss you. I'll miss playing being married to you."

That about broke Sadie's heart, for in truth, she had never considered it playing. Feeling completely hopeless, she pulled Martha close, ignoring the pain in her back and shoulders. Martha tipped back her head, and Sadie bent to kiss her with all the feeling she could. She slid her tongue into Martha's waiting mouth. They had never kissed that way before. Sadie nearly changed her mind about going right then and there.

From a nearby tree came the hoot of an owl, causing them both to jump. Their spell was snapped and they broke apart.

Sadie was as jumpy as a treed coon and scared plenty about going and about Pa being turned loose and coming after her with his double-barrel shotgun. She stepped back from Martha, knowing she was letting go of the most holy thing in her life.

"Will you be back?" Martha asked. Her voice

trembled like an aspen leaf, and she was beginning to cry hard.

"I don't think so," Sadie answered honestly. "But I'll for sure never forget you."

Martha didn't say anything more as Sadie said, "Pa's in the barn tied up tight. You got to tell my ma to cut him loose or he'll freeze to death by morning. And then you and your ma leave right away. No telling what Pa might do once he's free." Although Sadie had a pretty good idea of what he'd do. He'd grab his gun, whistle to his hound and then come looking for her.

She had to leave right this second, and she would have if Martha hadn't reached out and laid her small hand along Sadie's cheek.

"Oh, Martha." She sobbed. Wincing with pain, she grabbed her love in one final embrace, giving her one last desperate kiss before tearing herself away from Martha's clinging arms. "I love you, Martha. I surely do. I will forever and ever. Never forget that old Sadie loved you first."

"I won't." Martha was sobbing too, and grabbing Sadie again, trying to latch herself around Sadie's waist. She laid her head against Sadie's chest. "I love you, too, Sadie. You treated me like a man should treat a woman. I'll always love you best for that."

One final look at Martha and Sadie began running down the road, sobbing as she did.

She heard Martha call after her as she fled, "Please don't go, Sadie. *Please!*" But Sadie just didn't have it in her to stay home anymore.

159

Chapter Seventeen
Sadie, 1872

It had been a very bad day for Sadie Riley. It was nearing sundown and she hadn't yet eaten. She hadn't eaten yesterday, either, or the day before that. That was the day her food had run out, and she didn't dare fire her rifle out here on the open Kansas plains and maybe draw someone's unnecessary attention. She still had a smidgen of water left in her canteen, but she couldn't go far on that and no food.

Her horse was also in terrible shape. His ribs

were beginning to show more than they should have, and his eyes had lost their alertness. His fine bay coat was dusty and dull. He'd pick at the grass in the evenings when they cold-camped for the night, but the sun had been unmerciful all summer and the grass was burnt back and dried out. Not having had any water for three days except what Sadie could take from her canteen and rub on his nose for him to lick made him sluggish.

She was feeling a whole lot older than her twenty years. She ached all over from five straight days of riding, and her ass 'bout busted from the saddle. But she figured on riding for another hour anyway, just in case there was somebody out there who would let her water her horse. If she didn't run into somebody by then — a soddy, ranch, anything — she'd quit for the day.

Taking off her slouch hat, she wiped her brow with a red bandanna she pulled from the rear pocket of her canvas pants and observed how the land lay flat as a griddle cake except for the slight rise she'd been climbing for the past hour. The hill wasn't much to speak of, but it blocked the next fifty miles or so from view. She crested the rise in another fifteen minutes and was so grateful for what lay before her that she cried for the first time since leaving home two years ago. On the downside of the sloping land, just where the earth leveled off, sat a ranch. She gave thanks to whatever was out there to give thanks to and dried her tears. No sense in wasting what little water she had left in her on useless tears.

Beyond the immediate area, there looked to be around two thousand head of cattle. There was probably even more beef out there, but the sun had dipped so low she couldn't see it.

A little less than an hour later she cautiously approached the house. It was a well-built place with a long porch attached. Sadie was partial to porches. She'd sat on one a long time ago in some rat-infested river town or other along the Mississippi's east side where she'd worked a spell, cleaning saloons and sleeping in a stable, taking care of horses till she could get herself a good horse and saddle. It was there that she'd sat on her first porch, in a porch swing, alongside a real pretty lady who'd taken a fancy to Sadie, completely believing that she was a young man. Sadie courted her until it was kissing time. When it came to that, she did like always. She lit out of town not daring to go any further than sitting on a porch or taking a stroll with a woman. That was it for old Sadie Riley.

She dismounted and threw her reins over a hitching rail. A lady in a white linen dress and looking fine as Sunday came out on the porch, saying, "I thought I heard a rider. Howdy, there."

Sadie peeled her tongue from the top of her mouth where it'd clove fast from dryness and croaked, "Howdy."

"Well, now," the lady in the fine linen dress said. "Ain't you a poor, ragged-looking thing, and riding a horse that should've been put down a long time ago. Guess you been on the trail a while."

"A while." Sadie remained in the saddle. She'd learned that men who moved too quickly scared womenfolk.

"Well, if you care to rest up, I got hot coffee, hot biscuits, fresh corn and potatoes and gravy and steak

—if you'd care to have some. Got canned peach pie, too."

"Water would be fine, ma'am. For my horse. Ain't looking for a handout."

"Proud one, huh?"

"Proud enough."

"Water it is, then. Take your horse over there to the trough. Let him drink his fill, then come on back so's I can say a proper good-bye before you go on your way."

"Yes, ma'am."

While her horse drank his fill, Sadie did too, and dunked her head in the water up to her flannel shirt collar. She pushed back her hair; it was long and in real bad shape. She'd cut it off tomorrow with her knife and start short again. It was too damned hot for long hair. She filled up her canteen and tried to neaten herself up some, brushing off her shirt and pants. There wasn't anything she could do to improve the looks of her worn-down-at-the-heels, scuffed-up boots.

Putting on her hat, she returned to the house. The lady came out with a heaping plate of food. "Can't eat all this by myself, and my man is off on the range. Hate to waste it on the chickens." Sadie hadn't seen any chickens.

"Thank you, ma'am. I'll help you, then. Can't stand waste, myself." She sat on the edge of the porch and wolfed down the food.

"Care for some pie?"

"Thank you, ma'am. A piece would suit me fine."

The woman took Sadie's dish with her and when she returned she brought a quarter piece of pie on a serving dish. Sadie wolfed that down, too.

"I ain't never seen a woman go about in men's clothing before," the lady said. "What name do you go by?"

"I ain't no woman, ma'am." Sadie was gonna have to ride. Now. "Sorry I can't talk to you none about woman stuff. Must get lonely out here by yourself. You ought to get you some children."

"Been thinking on it."

Sadie touched the brim of her hat. "Evening, ma'am, and thank you."

The lady stepped off the porch and walked up to Sadie. "I say you're a woman."

She put her hand on Sadie's small breast before Sadie could react. Sadie grabbed her wrist, saying, "You got no call to do that, ma'am."

"I'm right."

"Don't matter. I'm moving on."

"Anybody else know?"

Sadie mounted up. "No, ma'am, and I'd be obliged if you didn't let on to folks."

"You need a job? I need a cook real bad. I hate like hell to cook."

"Ladies don't cuss, ma'am, and no, I don't need a job."

"Get down, miss."

"Evening, ma'am." Again Sadie touched her hat and turned to go.

She heard the lady go into the house and then come right back out again. She heard the door slam and she heard the shot and the bullet whiz past her ear. Sadie sawed on the reins, trying to steady her startled mount.

"Next one'll drop you. Now get out of that saddle and come sit on this here porch."

Sadie had never been shot at before, and it scared her plenty. Not only that, the lady was damn good with that rifle. She brought her horse around. "Whatever you say, ma'am."

"Chair, here."

Sadie dismounted and took a ladderback next to the woman, watching her set the gun inside the house.

"Now," the woman began, "my name's Gertrude Sharp, married to Carl Sharp recent from Missouri. What's your name?"

Sadie took off her hat and dropped it beside her. She wasn't all that sure she wasn't asleep and dreaming, so tired was she. "Henry Jones, ma'am."

"What's your lady's name?"

"I don't use it no more, ma'am."

"Call me Gert. I ain't but fifteen and don't deserve being called ma'am, yet. Makes me sound old."

"Yes, ma'am — Gert."

"Didn't hear your name yet."

Sadie slapped her hands on her thighs. "Had to think a minute, Gert, ain't heard it in so long. It's Sadie Riley. Call me Henry."

"I'll call you Sadie. It's a pretty name. You ought not to be burying it. Why you dressed up like a man, Sadie Riley?"

"You ask a lot of questions. Now I'm gonna ask you one. How's it you know how to shoot like a man?"

"My husband taught me."

Sadie stretched her long legs out before her and pulled a tobacco pouch from her breast pocket. Expertly, she rolled a smoke then stuffed the pouch away. "Well, Gert, I travel alone. Can't do that if I'm dressed like a woman." She struck a match on the bottom of her boot and drew deep on the cigarette, then blew herself several perfect rings before inhaling again.

"I still need a cook. How about taking the job. Move on when you're sick of it."

"That might be tomorrow — providing I take the job."

"You'll take it. You're hungry enough. What do you cook?"

"Anything you like." Sadie had learned all about cooking from a peddler she'd partnered up with for a spell some time ago. She'd thought she'd hate it but discovered she had a pretty good hand at fixing up a tasty meal.

They walked to the barn together to stable Sadie's horse and continued chatting on the porch until after midnight. Gert learned that Sadie had been moving south and southwest for the past two years. She had chopped wood, cleared and plowed fields, helped build a schoolhouse and a church, but she never returned home.

By the time Sadie quit speaking, telling Gert more than she'd ever told anyone else, she'd fallen in love with the young woman. She'd be taking the job, all right, just to be near such a fine lady all dressed up in snow-white linen and looking pretty as a pic-ture, what with her black hair and dark eyes and tiny frame. Sadie was partial to small women. It made her feel strong when she stood next to them.

Gert's being only fifteen years old didn't mean very much as Sadie listened to her talk about the ranch, what it needed to grow, the politics of the day, women's lot in life and how she thought children ought to be raised. Way she talked, she sounded like she was twenty or better. She had a real good head on her shoulders for being so young, Sadie thought.

Sadie started cooking for the Sharps the following morning and Gert began sewing Sadie a dress and wouldn't let her see it before it was done. Sadie thought Gert took more measurements than a body needed for a dress. "It ain't going to be a wedding gown, Gert," Sadie told her.

"Maybe not, Sadie Riley, but you ought to look pretty all the same. Get that hair of yours washed, too."

It wasn't long before the two women became fast friends. Carl liked Sadie, too. He'd learned that if he needed an extra hand mending fences, castrating bull calves or swinging a hammer, Sadie knew what to do and how to do it well.

During the passing weeks, Gert came to mean more and more to Sadie. Almost every evening after she had finished up in the kitchen for the day, her still smelling like pies and cakes and fresh-roasted meat, the sweat pouring down her face like she'd just jumped in a creek, and Gert in her finery looking like a rose and smelling like one, too, they would talk about little things as they watched the day turn from pink to orange to rust red and finally to black. They listened to the coyotes singing to the moon as they rocked away the miles in a couple of rockers Carl had sent off to Chicago for.

Since that first night, Sadie slept in the big house

down the hall from Gert and Carl. She was a light sleeper and knew every time Carl made love to his wife. During those times, Sadie would slip out of bed and go sleep in the barn. She couldn't stand hearing Carl and Gert grunting and moaning like animals. Like Pa on top of Ma. Like her on top of Martha. The memories were too sorrowful to endure. She slept fitfully, tossing and turning and finding a saddle for a pillow mighty uncomfortable. She'd return to her room just before daybreak, and far as she could tell, her employers never knew she had left the house.

One evening as she and Gert routinely settled each in her favorite rocker, Gert said wistfully and with a great sigh, "I wish Carl would let me go with him on those trail rides of his. I did a lot of riding when we came down the Santa Fe Trail this past year. I know how to ride with the best of them, but he wants me to stay home and be a lady now. It gets pretty boring sometimes when he's gone for months at a time."

For several days following, Sadie thought about what Gert had said. One afternoon she was up to her elbows in flour, preparing enough bread dough to bake fifteen loaves for the coming weekend. Gert came in and sat at a fine cherry table her mother had sent along with the newlyweds. Sadie hadn't been able to come up with a good way to hint to Gert what was on her mind. She'd just have to come out and say it.

"Got coffee here if you'd like some," she said to get herself going.

"Blacker than hell," Gert said, the way she always

did. "Gimme a cookie there, too, will you?" Gert pointed to the cookie jar. "And sit with me a while. You look all done in."

Sadie brought over the jar, then poured each of them coffee. She drew out a sugar cookie and bit into it. "I been thinking, Gert. We could go off by ourselves if you want to get away from here sometime."

Gert leaped up and came around the table to grab Sadie's arm. "You mean that, or are you just talking?"

"I'm meaning it. I could take care of you."

"I don't know that I need taking care of, but I'd love to go."

"Better ask Carl."

"He ain't here to ask and won't be for three months or better." But then, Sadie already knew that. "There's just his foreman here to boss the place, and I ain't gonna ask no bowlegged, downright ornery, tobacco-spittin', meaner'n hell cowboy if I can go off by myself for a while."

"I take it you don't value his opinion much."

"Never have and never will. But Carl trusts him, so I suppose when it comes to cows he knows what he's talking about." Gert sat again and took a hearty swig of coffee. She spit out what she didn't swallow. The coffee flew across the table. "Jesus Christ, woman. This ain't coffee, it's coal tar."

"You said strong."

"I said black."

Nonplussed, Sadie bit into her cookie. "Same thing."

"It ain't."

"Okay, it ain't. Then, Mrs. Sharp, as lady of this

here house and wife of the owner, and Mr. Sharp gone off and all, I guess you got to make this decision all by yourself."

"Guess I do." Gert eyes were full of mischief. "I say we move out tonight." She emptied her cup and the pot out the back door.

Sadie put down her cookie and threw up her hands. "Now hold on there, Gert. This ain't no military campaign we're going on. It's just moving around some, relaxing and enjoying ourselves."

Their traveling started like that. When Carl left, so did the two women, with Gert sometimes wearing Carl's clothing so she could ride a horse without restriction. Once they took a train to Missouri to visit Gert's parents. Most times they took the wagon traveling just far enough away from the house while remaining close enough to be safe from Indians or white men. They were always back before Carl was.

Following their first outing, as soon as Carl returned, his foreman informed him of Mrs. Sharp's absence. "You were safe because Sadie was with you," Carl said angrily to his young, wayward wife. "She's half-man, anyway. Now, I want you staying right on this ranch until I get back."

His comment angered Gert. She'd had no idea he looked down upon Sadie for her unusual approach to living, and she'd argued hard and long, she later told Sadie, to convince him that she had been perfectly safe on her first trip without his permission, and she damn well would be safe on any trip with Sadie Riley along. She badgered him for five days before he finally relented.

Meanwhile, Sadie stayed out of his sight, hiding in the kitchen until he went to bed.

"There lots about me Carl don't know, anymore," Gert said to Sadie one night as they lay out on the prairie. "And I ain't planning on telling him either."

Sadie nodded, grinning. "All's I know is that you make me an awful happy woman. I'd be liking to stay right here with you for the rest of my life."

It was too damn bad that Carl lived there, too.

Chapter Eighteen
Laurie, 1960

"Hmm. So Grandma had a woman lover at one time — Henry."

"I don't know. Grandma never said."

"Sure sounds it to me."

"Couldn't say."

Ev could if she wanted to. What was the big secret if Grandma Gertie took up with a girl? The woman was dead. The affair happened decades ago.

"And the drawing of the four of them standing by a lake in those beautiful gowns."

"All in Helena's imagination."

"Sadie seemed to have done quite well," Laurie said. "Why'd she end up in that asylum?"

Ev rolled over next to her. "Circumstances."

"What happened? Did Carl discover them? That seems to be the pattern here. Women making love to other women. Being discovered by some uncomprehending male. You aren't exactly painting a very rosy picture of women loving women, or of the men in their lives."

"At that time? No, I'm not. Times have changed."

"I wouldn't know, and I'm surprised that you would."

"Maybe I'm just hoping for the best," Ev said. "Do you want to hear the rest of Sadie's story?"

"Briefly."

"Grandma got pregnant. She told me that Sadie couldn't take it and just picked up and moved on further west one day. She told me Sadie broke her heart in two."

"But wait a minute," Laurie said after a moment's thought. "I'm assuming that Louisa and Helena got together, and if the four of them, that is Honora and Sadie, too, always sat together at the same table, then did Sadie take up with Honora or was there somebody else you haven't told me about yet?"

"Sadie became Honora's lover."

"Good old Sadie. She did get around, didn't she? How long did this one last?"

"Until death did they part." Ev lay on her back, lazily watching the rolling clouds passing overhead.

"And when exactly was that?"

"When they grew old. Right there in the asylum. None of them were ever released."

"None? Ever?"

Ev shook her head.

"But making love in so public a place. How . . . where . . ?"

"Here and there. Whenever and wherever they could find the opportunity."

Laurie shook her head in dismay. "How sad, how tragically sad. To have lived and died like that. There. Trapped. And poor Sadie."

"It's something, isn't it? And yet they were still able to give each other complete loyalty and devotion." Ev looked squarely into Laurie's eyes. "That's what I believe love is. Grandma once told me about two old lovers of twenty-nine years in there, who committed double suicide after they were found out. You want to hear that story?"

"No!"

Ev rolled onto her side and commenced to brush grass from her hip. "Maybe it wasn't so bad for them. It's true, they did all love women. Very much. It cost them, but they were willing to pay the price. That has to mean something."

"But, Sadie. She was certainly free to go her own way. She never married."

"But she did."

"I don't believe it."

"She married. Right in a church. Then that night the lady saw that Sadie was a woman, not a man."

"Lady? Are you telling me she had the audacity to marry another woman?"

"Yup."

174

"But obviously it didn't last." Laurie would have liked to know that at least one of the women ended up being happy even if she was queer.

Ev sat up, folding her arms around her knees. "First they tarred and feathered her. Sadie, I mean."

Impatiently, Laurie waved away Ev's irrelevant comment. "They actually did this to a woman?"

"While she was buck naked. Then they hanged her, but the rope snapped. They . . ."

"Who's this 'they' you keep mentioning?"

"They, the men, and some women too. Including the humiliated and outraged bride, who was especially vicious to Sadie." Laurie had no intention of asking in what way the bride retaliated. The answer was sure to be excruciating enough to avoid learning about for now. "Anyway," Laurie continued, "they thought her life being spared was a sign from God. Sadie was not supposed to die, but rather live to think about how evil and vile a creature she was, all day long, every day, for the rest of her life."

"So they packed her up and shipped her off to an insane asylum. One far, far away."

"Best thing they could have done for her. Women all over the place." Ev chuckled. "She had several lovers before she settled permanently on Honora."

Laurie thoughtfully watched an ant crawling over her boot and tapped a finger against her lips. "I wonder what it's like — making love to a woman." The tapping continued. "I wonder what they . . . I mean, how do they have intercourse? I mean . . . how *can* they?"

"Don't you mean, how can we?"

Laurie noticed Ev watching her from the corner of her eye. "You mean, you and me?"

175

"No, we. We women. You keep saying, 'How can they?' 'They' are 'we.' You keep making 'they' sound like something apart from yourself. You're a woman, too."

"Yes, but I don't sleep with . . ."

"Never?"

"Of course not, Ev. What do you think I am?"

Ev said, barely above a whisper, "I wouldn't want to make love *to* a woman. I'd want to make love *with* her."

Laurie jumped to her feet, agitated and restless. She brushed off the seat of her pants. "I think it's time we left."

"Would you like to?"

"This minute."

Ev stood then, too. Laurie studied her most cherished friend for a moment. So cute, so tiny, Laurie thought. She loved holding Ev in her arms because of her small size. Ev's head tucked very neatly beneath Laurie's chin. Sadie had felt the same way toward Martha. Laurie started for her horse.

Ev remained where she was, her words turning soft, trembling a bit. "I don't mean leave. I mean make love . . . with me . . . to . . . to find out."

"*Ev!*" Laurie spoke sharply, too sharply, perhaps, but Ev certainly knew her better than to ask such a question as that! And why did she just keep standing there looking at her as though she, Laurie, had been the unreasonable one? "Ev, let's go." Again the sharpness. Again she regretted her tone. But she just couldn't deal with this.

"You're afraid," Ev said.

"I am not afraid, Eveleen. I'm just not inclined."

Their gazes clashed, neither of them yielding for

176

several long seconds until Ev asked, "A kiss then? One?"

Laurie whirled in exasperation, her arms reaching outward to the world as if to say, "What am I going to do with this woman?"

She strode to her mount and stopped, her hand on the horn, her body ready to swing into the saddle. She felt like a rubber band stretched beyond capacity.

She closed her eyes, inhaling deeply, and leaned her forehead against the warm, smooth fender of the saddle. Her hand dropped to the stirrup as she faced her friend. "All right, Ev. One kiss. One." She could stand that. What was a single kiss? Laurie got plenty from Joe. Ev apparently got none from anyone. Maybe a kiss would ease some of her pain regarding the loss of her grandmother. Maybe that was all Ev needed.

Laurie didn't have to move. Ev came to stand by her side. She quite surprised Laurie, who was prepared to be kissed immediately, quickly, and have it done and over with. Instead, Ev rested her face against Laurie's chest and reached up to wrap her arms around her neck.

As uncomfortable as Laurie was with understanding just what her best friend was, or thought she was, Laurie pulled Ev close to her while holding herself rigidly erect, her head tipped slightly away from Ev's hair. She had always loved the outdoorsy smell of Ev. Always so healthy, so full of life. But at that moment she didn't want to savor the sweet scent of Ev's shampoo, didn't want to smell the sweat of her body from today's labors. Not right now, she didn't. It threatened her sense of self, of who she was, who she had always been.

Ev drew a deep breath. Laurie heard her exhale in a long sigh, felt her relax. She breathed easily, steadily, while Laurie, wound like a clock spring, waited for Ev to make her move.

Two or three minutes passed before Ev raised her face to Laurie. Those beautiful blue eyes, she thought. Her heart raced. She could feel it pounding against Ev's chest. *Thump, thump, thump.*

"Are you afraid, Laurie?" Ev asked.

Laurie scoffed. What had she to be afraid of? "Don't be silly."

"That's good," Ev said, again laying her head against Laurie's chest. "I can hear your heart pounding. You have a good, strong heart."

Seconds passed, years, decades, before Ev looked up again. She moved slowly and Laurie was grateful for that. Any sudden moves, and she knew she would all but panic. Good old Sadie knew what she was talking about. She had understood women well. Ev placed her hands against Laurie's cheeks, paused, then very slowly drew Laurie's face to her own.

Laurie allowed herself to be guided to Ev. Ev moved her lips against Laurie's, and Laurie allowed her teeth to be separated and her tongue to be caressed by Ev's.

Unconsciously, Laurie's lips moved. When she realized it, she stopped as Ev kept her mouth poised upon Laurie's.

Ev was so very much in need of being held, loved, protected. I can do this, Laurie thought. I can give this kiss in a meaningful, loving way to this woman who needs it right now, who trusts me and chose me long ago as her best friend. It is only a kiss. Nothing more is expected.

That settled, she threw herself into the act, pulling Ev tight, bearing down on her mouth the way Joe bore down on hers, moving her tongue over Ev's teeth the way Joe did, and to the roof of Ev's mouth.

Ev made sounds, soft sounds, womanly sounds that were delightful to hear. Laurie took concealed pride in being able to make Ev respond to her like that. She felt powerful, in control of herself and of being willing to give — no, to share this unusual gift with Ev.

So this was what Joe experienced when he held her, she thought, when he molded himself against her, tucked her head beneath his chin. Lucky Joe. She would love to be able to hold him that way. Now, wasn't that an absurd thought? She didn't want to cuddle some man like one would a child.

My, but Ev did feel very — holdable.

And then their kiss ended.

Ev stepped away. Laurie put her hands on Ev's shoulders as Ev retreated, the two women remaining in contact, arms outstretched as Laurie's fingers trailed the length of Ev's arms until only their fingertips touched. Feeling an inexplicable wrenching in her chest, Laurie dropped her hands to her sides.

"And about making love . . ." Ev said, her eyes wide and honest.

"Oh, now wait a minute, Ev. We weren't going to go that far."

"Tonight, after dinner, when the sun has set. There's going to be a full moon. We could put on some soft music, have a glass of wine."

"I simply can't, Ev. I've never slept with a woman. I don't know what they do in bed. You've had lots of women. I'd be embarrassed, clumsy. I'm

179

just not that way. Please try to understand. You should find somebody, someone else who's ..." Her voice trailed off. She felt weak, exposed, without resources against Ev's request.

"I remind you, Laurie, the 'they' you speak of is us. 'They' are women. No different from you."

"Well, you know what I mean. *They* are lesbians. I'm not."

"Around nine. My room. Too many bugs outside at night."

"But, Ev ..." Laurie was almost pleading.

"Just to try. It isn't like I'm asking you to become an ax murderess. Where's the harm?"

"But I just would not know what to do. You do! I'd feel stupid. Stupid!"

Laurie was unable to read anything into Ev's face as Ev walked over to Mr. Big Bucks and mounted up. The stallion performed his usual antics as she rammed her feet into the stirrups and grabbed the horn for stability. She cantered off, leaving Laurie to chase after her.

For the rest of the day, nothing more was said about their talk — or their kiss. They headed for the west pasture four miles away, joining two cowhands repairing fences and swearing up a storm at the hated job. She and Ev had planned to help the men, but instead ended up just sitting around and talking with them.

At noon, the cooks bantered with the two women, but only Ev responded, laughing and bedeviling them, too, and eating as though it might be her final meal. Laurie ate little, having other things on her mind.

Casually, Ev said, "I'll be out on the range with

Dad until suppertime or later. Why don't you take a walk or a nap?"

Laurie agreed. A nap would do her good. It would also give her time to consider how she might talk with Ev about her misguided hopes for this evening. She didn't want to hurt Ev, but maybe she could explain why it wasn't a good idea.

The afternoon was quiet with Ev and Luke, who was seldom seen except for meals, gone and the cooks busy in the kitchen. Feeling a bit at loose ends, Laurie wandered around the house. For the first time since Grandma's death, she entered the deceased woman's bedroom. The place gave her an eerie feeling, as though Grandma were still alive. So far everything in there remained undisturbed.

She looked at the drawing on the bureau. "I know a lot about you people, how strong you were, how loyal and dedicated to one another. Maybe that's the lesson Grandma was trying to teach me. But you probably would have married or never taken up with a woman if you'd had the chance to be free or to stay with your husband, Honora, as was your case, and if he'd been a decent man."

"Not true, Laurie."

"Ev, I though you were gone." She looked toward the doorway. Ev must have gone into her bedroom. "Wait. I thought you were going with your dad." Ev wasn't in her room.

Irritated that Ev would play silly games like this, Laurie stepped out onto the porch, intending to tell her about it. Pauline and Miriam were the only ones there, taking a needed break as they quietly rocked together, chatting and smoking.

Laurie looked both ways for Ev. Exasperated, she frowned again and put her hands on her hips. "Either one of you see which way Ev went?"

Miriam pointed north. "That way, 'bout half an hour ago."

"No, she's here somewhere. I just heard her inside. She came this way."

"Well," Pauline drawled, "I saw her ride off with Luke a while ago, right up that rise."

Tight-lipped, Laurie went back inside and searched the house for Ev. Not finding her, Laurie returned to Grandma's room and picked up the drawing, staring at each woman for a very long time. "So, you're back. Which one of you spoke to me a minute ago? You all look guilty as hell to me. You scare me and you've been dead for years. You're supposed to be gone from here, Ev said. But you're not. Or . . . was it you I heard, Grandma?"

She half-expected an answer. Receiving none, she replaced the drawing and went to her room. She slept until evening.

Chapter Nineteen

"It's way past suppertime, Laurie." Ev stood beside the bed. "Want something to eat?"

"Something cold to drink would be good." Laurie felt like she'd been eating cotton balls. "Maybe a shower, too."

"I'll be in the kitchen." As Ev left, Laurie headed for the bathroom. She first showered beneath the coldest water she could bear before switching to hot, then back to cold once more. She washed her hair, sensing the thick cobwebs dissipating from her disorderly mind. Donning a short, fresh sundress, she headed for the kitchen.

"Lemonade? Iced tea? Coffee?" Ev offered.

"Lemonade. Tangy enough to curl my toes."

"Right." Ev placed a sweating glass of amber liquid before her along with a plate of potato salad and sliced cucumbers and tomatoes. "Cold stuff, but light. Good on a hot night."

"Is it hot out?"

"Very. Good night to hang around inside, but I'm going to bed. See you in a bit." Abruptly, Ev left.

Laurie had only partially eaten her salad and drunk her lemonade. She sat guiltily, unable to finish her meal, feeling obligated to follow Ev, to go to bed with her, to make love with her.

Her thoughts whirled for several minutes before she came to a decision. To hell with the whole idea. She wouldn't do it!

She headed for her own room and flipped on the light. Ev lay naked on the sheets, the covers cast aside. Small burning candles in tiny dishes had been placed around the room. Good to her word, Ev had a bottle of wine cooling in a bucket beside the bed. The radio was tuned to slow romantic tunes.

"Country candles," Ev said. Her eyes were soft, her voice calm and even.

"For Christ's sake, Ev." Laurie stared at her. As often as she had seen Ev nude, she'd never before noticed how beautiful she really was — all muscle, stomach flat and strong, breasts as tiny as could be without being too small.

Laurie sat slowly. Beside Ev. She reached out and tentatively stroked her hair. "You just never give up, do you?"

"No, I never do."

Laurie sighed softly. Joe would never understand this one. She wouldn't either. "Oh, God, what the hell. I'll join you." But it would be for Ev's sake, only. She doused the overhead light, plunging the bedroom into a warm glow. Shadows flickered on the walls and across the room. Lights danced in Ev's eyes. "You are a pretty thing, aren't you," Laurie said.

"I'd like you to think so."

"I do. I've always thought that."

"Let me undress you, Laurie."

"What if someone comes in here, Ev?" Laurie would die if that happened, and it easily could. There were no locks in the house. Not even on the front and back doors.

"Dad's gone up to Kinsley. I think he's got a girlfriend, so I doubt he'll be back tonight, and the cooks are in their rooms. I know they're already asleep. Unless there's a major storm, they won't wake up until morning."

"You certain?"

"They never have so far."

They both stood and Laurie, her heart pounding, raised her arms above her head and allowed Ev to remove her dress and then her bra. Her knuckles brushed against Laurie's stomach, setting her muscles into tight, quivering knots. She watched Ev lower her panties, leaving Laurie without a stitch to cover herself except for her sandals. Nervously she stepped out of them, then lay down, not knowing what else to do.

The sheets felt pleasantly cool against her skin. She caught the sweet scent of Ev's perfume, the fragrance just enough to send teasing tingles of pleasure stalking through her, like Joe's aftershave always did.

Ev stretched out beside her. "You are a long one. I admire tall women." She ran her hand over Laurie's shoulder.

Laurie let Ev nestle against her, uneasy but not frightened. "And how many might that be?"

"All of them."

"How many lovers have you had?" Laurie asked.

"None so far."

"None?"

"Not so far."

"But you said . . ."

"You assumed. People do that. Take a little word or two and make a whole story out of it." She rested her knee and an arm across Laurie's body.

"No women, none at all?"

"And no men. I've been waiting for you."

Laurie stared speechlessly at the ceiling. She whispered, "I never would have thought that."

"That time in college I went away. Remember?"

"The abortion. It never happened."

"That's right." Ev's fingers traced circles around Laurie's breasts. "I had to get away for a while. I couldn't stand being so close to you anymore. Day after day, night after night. Especially night. You were like a potion I needed to even draw breath each day. So I left. When I felt better, stronger, I came back. Grandma and Dad thought I was sick, too sick to even talk to you. That's what I told them. I'm sorry for that part."

Laurie tightened her hold on Ev. "I missed you. I

was scared." She began running her fingers through Ev's hair, then pressed her lips against its silkiness.

"I love you, Laurie," Ev whispered. "I have for years and years."

"I know. At least, now I know." Laurie kissed the top of Ev's ear.

"Why are you willing to love me tonight?"

Laurie took a deep, thoughtful breath. "I don't know. I wasn't going to. The idea frightened me. It's so foreign to anything I know."

"Me, too. Maybe more so. You've made love before. I haven't."

Laurie laughed lightly. "So I guess I'm the more experienced one after all, aren't I?"

"I'd say so. And will you kiss me?"

"Yes, Ev, dear, I'll kiss you. And we'll love each other all night long." She rose on her elbow and leaned over Ev's face. Her hair fell across her shoulders and onto Ev's. Their lips met, melding together, moving together, their tongues searching. Laurie kissed Ev's throat and breasts and then moved to her belly without qualms, without inhibitions. Ev rose to her kisses, pulling Laurie on top of her. "I'm too heavy, Ev."

"No, you're perfect." Ev positioned Laurie between her legs. She pressed against Laurie while pulling Laurie against her, guiding her with palms and fingers, grasping her hips and buttocks.

Laurie interpreted Ev's signals and moves. They became two dancers, Ev moving increasingly fast, Laurie keeping pace, reading her perfectly. She stayed with Ev until white heat scorched her, until she and

Ev became one person, one life, one heart beating — loving each other with absolute purity.

Afterward, they lay shaking, Laurie resting on Ev's body. Her chest filled with love and a deep longing to hold Ev like this all night long.

There were so many more things they could have done, so many more kisses, caresses, gazing into each others' eyes. Yet, Laurie felt, what she and Ev had shared had been perfect in every way. Another story created, Grandma, she silently whispered to the old woman.

She felt Ev drift off to sleep, then carefully slipped to her lover's side. Holding Ev was so different from being held by big Joe. She was glad that she and Ev had made love tonight. She was very, very glad.

She spent her days with Ev, lazily riding across the plains, searching for stray cattle, rocking the evenings away with Ev always by her side. There were no more nights of love or requests from Ev for more, nor were there any more stories. Ev was quiet, an excellent hostess and then, finally, the one who said good-bye first.

"I've loved it here, Ev," Laurie said. "I've learned a lot." She had said her good-byes to Luke last night, knowing he'd be up and gone before the sun rose.

Ev nodded.

"I'm sorry again, about Grandma. The place won't be the same without her."

Again Ev nodded. She took Laurie in her arms, holding her tightly. "I love you, Laurie."

"Yes," was all Laurie could think to say. She was the first to let go.

"Have a safe trip."

"I'll call when I get there."

"Sure." No tears.

Laurie drove away not looking back; she never looked back. She knew Ev was still on the porch watching her, and would be until she could no longer see Laurie's car or even its dust.

Laurie drove all that day and into the night, thinking about Ev and about Joe. By dawn she was sure that all the dust existing on this earth had purposely settled in her eyes alone. She rubbed them as she drove on, unable to bear the thought of stopping. If she did, she would have to be still, doing nothing. She wouldn't have to concentrate on keeping the car on the road, the gas to the floor, the brake at the ready.

She would have to think.

Late in the afternoon of the second day, she was forced to pull off at a rest stop. It was that or die, and she didn't want to die.

She rolled down the windows and slept for eight hours, undisturbed by other weary motorists also stopping to catch a nap. She awoke around ten P.M., went to the bathroom and washed her face with cold water, letting it drip from her skin as she returned to her car.

Behind the wheel again, she remained unmoving. She needed to get going, to put the goddamn key in the goddamn ignition and get the hell going. Wearily, she fumbled around the keyhole until she could slide the key into its slot.

"Shit!" she said. She draped her arms over the

189

wheel resting her head against them. What was
wrong with her? She should be happy to get back to
Joe, to her air-conditioned apartment, to work where
she could bitch at the students and they could bitch
at her. There was so much life, so much activity, so
much hustle and bustle on campus and around town
at night.

Such great fun — going out nights, parties, good
wine, dancing to good bands, the flashing, bright
lights. She and Joe occasionally drove miles from the
city just to watch the lights of Cleveland sparkling
against the black backdrop of the night sky.
Sometimes a star would fall as though giving a
special blessing to them, to the city they both loved.

She didn't move for thirty minutes, rolling these
thoughts over and over in her mind before shifting to
thinking about Ev and what exactly the little cowgirl
meant to her.

There were many times when she and Ev had
also watched the stars. Comets had fallen from the
sky. Kansas nights were every bit as beautiful as
Cleveland's. But there was little entertainment in
Kansas. Everyone made their own, if they had time.
It was such a different world back there.

So was making love.

Finally, *finally* she had reached a climax with
another person and at the same time, no less. She
hadn't had to finish the job herself. Job? Was having
an orgasm by oneself a job? Like work?

It hadn't been work with Ev. They had barely
touched each other, and yet Laurie had been so
completely fulfilled, so at peace, so lovingly shared
that ... Yes, she decided, she had been shared — not
used, or perceived as used, as so often was the case

with poor Joe. It had made all the difference in what had passed between her and Ev. She could easily love Ev like that a million more times.

She considered the idea. But then what? Eventually, they would become accustomed to each other. Not every night was going to be a night to remember. Besides, what would she do with her time? She couldn't follow Ev all over 150,000 acres of land and work alongside her. She didn't have the stamina and she really didn't want to. That left playing the wife. That wouldn't be such a bad idea if she could have free rein in the house. But she preferred that Ev come to Cleveland and live there. Then Laurie could see her whenever she wanted to, which at the moment seemed to be all the time. But Ev would never agree to that. She hated cities.

Laurie counted the days from the time she had left Ev to next year's vacation on the Sunrise Ranch. Next year she must remember to ask Ev whatever became of Mrs. A.

Every year, Joe asked her to go away with him for a week, but she never had. Not with the chance to see the beauty of Kansas — and Ev — for four straight, uninterrupted weeks. He was usually good about accepting her decision, except once when he really got mad and accused her of being a lesbian. She had broken out in laughter, and he saw the ridiculousness of his comment, taking her to bed right then and there. She agreed but wished she could finish the dishes first so that she didn't have to face them afterward. Maybe she was just too, too practical to be romantic. With Joe.

She made it back home the following evening. Joe had a gourmet supper, cold wine and a hot bubble bath waiting for her. In bed he was gentle and quick, twice. She was numb with fatigue and could only pretend that she was with him. Like always, she thought.

Weeks slid by as she threw herself back into her work, once again caught up in the rat race of college life and its demands. She had phoned Ev a couple of times. Their conversations were strained, but they gamely got through it, discussing mundane things and then hanging up.

More weeks passed, each day growing depressingly shorter while she grew increasingly busy with the coming holiday season. From her desk, she called home to tell Joe she'd be late this evening and then picked up two pieces of clean, bonded white letter-head.

Carefully, meticulously, she slipped a carbon sheet between them before rolling them into her typewriter. At the top right, she typed her address and the date, then addressed it to Dr. Ansel Williams, Dean of Cleveland Community College. Her fingers flew across the keys and she expelled a great sigh of relief as she began the body:

It is with deep regret that I must inform you of my decision to resign from ...